PUFF

SUPER GRAN

Everything is happening at once in Chistleton, and things are far from quiet. Young Willard is praying anxiously for a miracle on the cricket field, as the local lads look set for a terrible defeat. But defeat is far from the minds of the Scunner and his crew when they decide to polish up their nasty habits and enrol at the new college in town, the Crooks' College – where the best pupils are the biggest villains! The scheming headmaster is none other than Rott N. Scoundrel and suddenly there are villains everywhere, bursting with enthusiasm and desperate to learn new tricks. The Scunner is sent into town to gain some (nasty) work experience. Without really trying he (almost) robs a safe and looks set to ruin the annual Chisleton pigeon race, by entering a very unusual bird – some drastic action is needed to stop these criminal classes and restore life to normal for the terrified townsfolk. One little old lady steps forward to take up the challenge, and even the Scunner turns pale: Super Gran has come to the rescue and the trouble is only just beginning . . .

Forrest Wilson

SUPER GRAN
TO THE RESCUE

Illustrated by David McKee

based on TV scripts by Jenny McDade

PUFFIN BOOKS

Puffin Books, Penguin Books Ltd, Harmondsworth, Middlesex, England
Viking Penguin Inc., 40 West 23rd Street, New York, New York 10010, U.S.A.
Penguin Books Australia Ltd, Ringwood, Victoria, Australia
Penguin Books Canada Limited, 2801 John Street, Markham, Ontario, Canada L3R 1B4
Penguin Books (N.Z.) Ltd, 182–190 Wairau Road, Auckland 10, New Zealand

First published 1987

Made and printed in Great Britain by
Richard Clay Ltd, Bungay, Suffolk
Typeset in Baskerville

Contents

1 Super Gran Walks the Plank!

Edison was shocked to see what was happening to Super Gran – she was walking the plank! And, what was worse, she was being made to walk the plank!

The girl had been crossing part of Chisleton Common on her way to meet Super Gran when she spotted her in the distance, walking over a very narrow plank of wood which was stretched across a broad, fast-flowing stream. And surrounding her were about a dozen boys, six on each side of the plank, prodding her, from the safety of the banks of the stream, with long poles.

'They're trying to make her fall in the water,' she gasped. 'They're tormenting her! Stop!' she yelled.

But the wind blew her words away and no one heard her.

Then as she ran nearer the stream she saw that Super Gran had her arms bound to her sides and her legs tied together, so she wasn't so much walking the plank as 'hobbling' the plank.

'What're they doing to her?' she cried as she ran.

She was shocked. But she was even more shocked to see two men standing behind the boys, egging them on. And as she got nearer still she was positively horrified

to see that Willard was amongst the boys and, worse still, the two men were Inspector Muggins and PC Leekie of the Chisleton police, in their off-duty clothes.

'What on earth are they playing at? And what are they thinking of, doing that to poor old Super Gran?'

She couldn't help herself. She yelled out at the top of her voice as she got nearer, just as Super Gran was about three-quarters of the way across the plank, hopping slowly as she went.

'S U - P E R G R A N . . .!'

But her shout didn't have the intended result. Super Gran, distracted by its suddenness, lost her balance and teetered about on the plank as if about to fall off it into the raging stream. And the boys just seemed to prod her all the more with the poles!

'Oh-oh, I'm falling . . . Oh . . . oh . . . oh . . .'

However, after a few wobbling hops she managed to regain her balance and scrambled to the other side of the river, where the boys and the men cheered her. They untied her arms and legs and then she looked back across the river to see who it was who had shouted at her and distracted her attention and almost made her fall into the water.

'Havers, lassie, what were you shouting at? You nearly had me in the river, so you did.'

Edison, crossing the plank to join Super Gran and the others on the other side of the stream, was taken aback at this.

'*I* nearly had you in the river?' She was indignant. 'What d'you think those boys – and those policemen! –

9

were trying to do? And the boys were shoving you with poles, too!'

'Blethers, lassie. They were supporting me, in case I lost my balance.'

'Huh?'

Super Gran laughed. 'Och, but you didn't know what was going on, did you? I forgot you weren't in on the secret, with you being a lassie.'

'But you're a lassie too. Or at least you were at one time!'

'Aye, but you see lassies – apart from me! – aren't allowed to be in on the secrets of the Chisleton Boys' Club.'

'Boys' Club?'

'Aye. And that was me on their initiation test – to let me join the club. Or at least become an honorary member of it.'

'But what about those two?' Edison asked, pointing to Muggins and Leekie, now standing to one side with Willard and a group of boys around them.

'They're here to supervise the test 'cos they're officials of the club. And they were also here in case I fell in the water. Not that there was much chance of that!'

'No, not until I shouted at you,' Edison said, ruefully.

Muggins, Leekie and Willard left the others and approached Super Gran and Edison.

'The committee has agreed,' Muggins solemnly intoned, 'that you, Super Gran, have successfully passed your initiation test to become an honorary member of the Chisleton Boys' Club.'

Leekie whipped out of his pocket a rolled up, and slightly crumpled, certificate and presented it to her to commemorate the event, and declared:

'As an honorary member you can now be called on at any time to help the club if it's in trouble. Do you agree?'

'Jings, of course. And you know, Rupert Leekie, that I'd come to the club's help anyway, even if I wasn't a member. I'd help anyone – even without a certificate! But I'm certainly proud to have been accepted as an honorary "boy"!'

'And there can't be many of *them* around!' Edison joked.

Some of the boys now lifted the plank and carried it away, along with the poles, while Super Gran and Willard, their arms around each other's shoulders, walked off across the common with Muggins and Leekie, all 'boys' together.

'Hey, wait for me,' Edison shouted after them as she ran to catch up with them. 'Just because I'm not a boy or an "honorary" boy you don't have to ignore me! Humph!'

The Scunner paced up and down his billiard room, depressed.

'What's the matter, Uncle?' Tub asked, as he ate a sandwich.

'The matter, Tub, is that I'm a failure in life.'

'Oh, is that all?' Tub said, finishing the last bite.

'Yeah,' Cedric said, 'you're always going on about it.'

'Yeah,' Dustin agreed, grinning idiotically – as usual. 'You *are* a failure!'

The Scunner removed Dustin's hat and clobbered him, Tub and Cedric, in turn, over the head with it.

Then he explained: 'You see, lads, when I set out at an early age to be a crook my ambition was to be the best in the business and that means the best – in the world!' He sighed. 'But instead of that I feel more like the worst in the world . . .'

He stopped and waited for his men to deny this, but they didn't, they seemed to agree that he *was* the worst in the world!

He was peeved at this. He didn't want them to agree with him on *this* occasion but, before he could grab their cues and twist them round their necks, Tub changed the subject. He lifted his uncle's newspaper, the *Gangsters' Gazette*, and pointed to an advert which seemed to be written in gibberish.

'What does this ad mean, Uncle?' he asked. 'It looks like Greek or Latin – or Martian!'

'What're you blethering about, Tub?' the Scunner asked. 'Oh that? That's a code, a secret code.'

'What sort of code?' asked Tub.

'A code that only we gangsters know about.'

'But you're not a wee gangster,' Tub laughed, 'you're a fairly tall gangster.'

'Ho, very funny, Tub,' said the fairly tall gangster, who went on to explain:

'Some of the adverts in the *Gangsters' Gazette* are written in code so that anyone who's reading the paper who shouldn't be reading it, won't understand it. People like PC Leekie and Inspector Muggins and the rest of their polis . . . er . . . police pals. See? Clever, eh?'

He then got his code book out and laboriously translated the advert into English.

'What does it say?' Tub asked, excitedly.

'It says, Tub, that a certain member of the criminal fraternity, by name Rott N. Scoundrel, is opening a branch of his Crooks' College in Chisleton – today. And he promises to teach crooks how to operate really crookedly and how to improve their crooked skills and become really expert in their chosen profession.'

'So wot, Boss?' Cedric said.

'So wot . . . er . . . what?' the Scunner replied. 'So what about us all going down there to enrol in this College for Crooks? Huh? It could lead to me being the world's greatest crook, in time.'

'You mean – go back to school?' Dustin gasped.

'What d'you mean go *back*?' Cedric snorted. 'You never went to school in the first place! You were always bunkin' off.'

'Well you won't want to bunk off this school,' the Scunner assured them, as they left his house to go in search of the Crooks' College. 'You'll be eager to go, to learn things.'

2   Crooks' College

The Scunner and his men drove through Chisleton
until they reached a rather posh road full of large houses
which stood in their own grounds, surrounded by high
walls.

'Is it one of these, Uncle?'

'Aye, I think so, Tub. I'll check the address in the
advert.'

He stopped the car at the side of the road.

'That looks like the place,' he said, glancing up from
the newspaper at a house two or three hundred metres
away.

'Look,' said Tub, 'there's someone coming.'

He pointed through the windscreen at the small man
who was creeping furtively along beside the wall, so
close to it that he was rubbing his arm against it as he
went. He looked all around, trying hard not to be spotted.

'That's your typical, small-time Burglar Bill,' the
Scunner declared, with an air of authority. 'He looks
like one of the college's prospective pupils.'

Then Bill, as the Scunner called him, thinking that
no one had seen him, stopped at a green door in the
wall on the far side of the main gate. He fiddled with
the lock, opened the door and slipped through into the
grounds of the house.

Before the Scunner could move the car off, Tub pointed again. 'There's another one!'

A second man had emerged from a lane and was also creeping along towards the main gate and he too glanced about to make sure that he wasn't being observed. Then he reached up, grasped the top of the wall and hauled himself up and over, into the grounds.

'And that was your typical cat burglar,' the Scunner declared, from his vast knowledge of the criminal classes, adding condescendingly, 'small-time, of course.'

And he christened him Wally, not only because he climbed the *wall*, but also because he *was* a wally!

'They're both wallies,' he said, pointing to the main gate of the house. 'Imagine not casing the joint first and spotting the gate lying wide open! The idiots could've walked straight in!'

He felt rather superior as he switched on the ignition to start up the car and drive it through the open gateway. But it travelled only five metres along the road before spluttering and stopping, having run out of petrol.

'You buffoons,' he yelled, turning in his seat to hit all three of his men, in turn, with his hat. 'Imagine not filling her up with juice.'

Leaving the car parked at the side of the road, they walked in through the main gateway, smirking at their superiority at finding the gate open instead of breaking in, as Bill and Wally had done. And as they walked along the driveway they were pleased to see the two men being apprehended by a large, severe-looking man dressed in a headmaster's outfit of black gown, mortarboard and old school tie, whose emblem was prison arrows! This, they realized, was Rott N. Scoundrel himself.

'Why did you break in through the green door?' he asked Bill. 'All you had to do was walk in through the open gateway.'

'That's what *I* said, didn't I?' The Scunner turned to his men for confirmation.

Then Scoundrel reprimanded Wally. 'And why did you climb over the wall? You should've checked the gate first – it was open.'

'See?' the Scunner said, in triumph.

'You should both have strolled in through the gates,' Scoundrel went on.

'As *we* did,' the Scunner interrupted, proudly.

'That was your first lesson at Rott N. Scoundrel's Crooks' College,' the man continued, ignoring the Scunner's comments.

'And *we* won't need that lesson,' the Scunner said, still feeling superior.

But then Scoundrel turned his attention to him and his men.

'You had no right walking in like that,' he said, wagging a finger at them admonishingly. 'You should have done what these other two did, and entered furtively! You should have forced a lock, or climbed the wall!'

So *none* of Scoundrel's would-be pupils could win, it seemed!

He then led all six of them towards the house. As they approached it a small wiry man came running out of the shrubbery. He pulled a jemmy out of his pocket and began attacking one of the window frames with it, intent on breaking in.

But before he got far the frame fell out, crashed down over his head and landed on his shoulders like a motor-racing champion's laurel wreath! But although he flinched when this happened, fearing the flying fragments which could injure him, there was no sound of breaking glass. This puzzled him *and* the on-lookers, who had stopped on their way, to watch this incident.

'The glass was removed and you could have gained entrance without trying to break in!' Scoundrel told his latest pupil.

'Huh?' he said, lifting the frame off his shoulders and tossing it to the ground in disgust.

'You'd only to climb in through the open space!'

Scoundrel turned to include all seven pupils. 'You've all heard of open prisons, haven't you? Well this is an open college. And I'm "'opin'" you'll enrol in it!'

He chuckled and led them into the building as the Scunner said:

'I'm gonna call that last guy "Windy".'

'Why "Windy", Uncle?' Tub asked, puzzled.

'Because he was trying to get in through the

"windae",' the Scunner replied, and laughed at his Glasgow-type joke.

Inside the house, they were shown into a room arranged like an old-fashioned classroom, with old-fashioned desks, chairs and blackboards. Three other pupils already sat at their desks and the seven new-comers joined them, squeezing into the primary-school-sized seats!

Scoundrel introduced himself. 'Now, as you possibly know, I am Rott N. Scoundrel – but you can call me Rott N, for short.'

'As long as the lessons aren't Rott N!' the Scunner sniggered, as Scoundrel continued:

'The first item on the agenda is registration, but I don't want you to use your real names, just nicknames.' He pointed at the Scunner. 'What's yours?'

'I'll have a whisky!' he chuckled.

'Ho, very funny. I meant your nickname.'

'The Scunner,' Tub told him, before his uncle could answer.

'Right, and what's yours?' he asked Tub, as he entered the Scunner's name in his teacher's register.

'A shandy!' Tub giggled.

Scoundrel lifted a cane and thumped it down on Tub's desk, making him leap in the air, stop giggling and answer: 'T . . . Tub.'

'And yours?' he asked Cedric as he put the cane down again.

Cedric pointed to himself and Dustin and said: 'We're the Muscles.'

'Right, and yours?' He turned to the man whom the Scunner had named Bill, but before he could answer the Scunner cut in with:

'We call him Bill – short for Burglar Bill.'

'Right, that'll do,' Scoundrel said before the man could offer an alternative. 'So long as he's not in the *Old* Bill – the police, eh?' he laughed. 'We don't want any spies in our midst, do we?'

'Wot, me a police spy?' he denied indignantly. 'You've gotta be joking!'

'And we call that one,' the Scunner said, pointing, 'Wally, 'cos he climbed the wall. And that one's Windy, 'cos he . . .'

'Climbed in the "windae"! Yes, I heard your witticism, Scunner,' Scoundrel said. 'And what's your nickname?' he asked another man.

'Shorty.'

'And yours?' he asked two men sitting in adjacent seats.

'I'm Basher,' said one, 'and this is my brother, Crasher.'

'Right,' he said, 'let's get started. Your first lesson is practical safe-breaking. Follow me to the workshop.'

He left the classroom but his pupils didn't exactly rush to follow him. It took them some time to untangle their adult legs from their tight-fitting desks, cursing profoundly as they did so.

'Get into your tight wee desks, get out of your tight wee desks,' muttered the Scunner, 'get into your tight . . .'

'Scunner!' yelled Scoundrel, popping his head back into the classroom. 'What's the hold-up?'

'Something bank-robbers do!' he quipped.

Presently they were each crouched in front of a safe and their headmaster was instructing them on which knobs and dials to turn, and how to listen to the tumblers tumbling.

'Don't you use a stethoscope to hear the tumblers?' asked the Scunner. 'All the crooks on the telly do that.'

'By all means – if you're breaking into a doctor's safe!' Scoundrel laughed.

'Now, here's another way to do it,' he said, producing an acetylene torch and safety goggles, and proceeding to show the men how to use them.

He opened a large safe in a corner of the room and pulled out a pile of coins and banknotes.

'Now one of you can have a go at that,' he said. 'Let's see now . . .'

The Scunner volunteered, but he made a mess of it. The safe ended up as a scorched, crumpled heap while the coins inside fused together into a pile of blackened metal and the banknotes went up in smoke.

'Humph!' Scoundrel snorted. 'Luckily for you that was only kiddies' toy money, otherwise you'd have ruined a fortune. Right, let's have you back into the classroom for your next lesson.'

'Oh no,' the Scunner groaned, 'not back into those tight wee desks again! My knees are all bruised to bits.'

'What is the next lesson?' Cedric asked.

'Letter writing.'

22

'What?' the Scunner exploded. 'Who wants to learn how to write letters? *I* can write letters! *Everyone* can write letters! What's writing letters to do with being a crook?'

'But the ones I'm going to teach you to write,' Scoundrel said, 'are ransom letters! To be used after you kidnap someone!'

3 Snobbers – and Scoundrels!

Super Gran entered Chisleton Park and headed towards the old, dilapidated, wooden cricket pavilion where Willard and the Boys' Club cricket team sat on the rickety steps, looking miserable. They were dressed in their whites – but they had the blues!

'What's the matter, Willie? You look as if someone's stolen your tattie scone!'

'Oh, hello, Gran,' he replied, looking up. 'We're waiting to play our match with the Snobbers Boys' Club.'

He was so depressed he didn't even ask what a tattie scone was!

'Aw, it's starting to drizzle.' She held her hand up to feel the rain, thinking that that was the reason for their misery.

'It's not that, Gran,' he explained. 'The Snobbers are terrific players and we don't stand a chance.'

'Yeah,' his pal added, 'and they're all big lads, too!'

'That's them now,' Willard said as a white minibus drove into the park and approached the pavilion. 'Wow! They've even got their own transport!'

Signs on the sides of the vehicle read: 'The Snobbers Boys' Club (For the Gentle Sons of Gentle Men), Poshtown'.

It stopped and its passengers alighted, wearing top

hats and looking every inch the 'gentleboys' they reckoned they were, including the disdainful looks they gave the mere mortals who were waiting to play them at cricket.

The first one out of the bus, their captain, held his hand up, felt the drizzling rain which was now increasing and produced a large white umbrella to shelter under. Black letters on it proclaimed: 'Snobbers – the Boys' Club Cricket League Champions'.

'I'm telling you,' Willard moaned as he reluctantly got to his feet, 'we don't stand a chance.'

'They look as if they were all born with silver spoons in their mouths,' said Super Gran.

'And with cricket bats in their hands,' Willard muttered. 'They've been top of the cricket league for years. No one's ever beaten them.'

'And look at the size of 'em,' his pal added.

All eleven players were tall and broad, and they dwarfed the Chisleton boys.

'They all look rich,' Willard said.

'Aye, I'm sure their fathers are all big city financiers, tycoons and bankers, with loads of money,' Super Gran agreed.

They looked extremely confident as they swaggered towards the pavilion, smirking, while Willard's team all looked rather depressed. The Snobbers looked like cricketers and they would play like cricketers once they changed into their whites, which would probably make the Chisleton team's whites look grubby by comparison.

Pennants were exchanged between the teams. But whereas the Chisleton one was a tatty old cloth thing, the one which the Snobbers presented was made of gold cloth, with a crest of silver.

'I'm Willard Smith,' Willard said as he handed over his pennant. 'Captain of the Chisleton Boys' Club cricket team.'

'And I am Timothy Toff,' the Snobbers' captain replied, as he snootily took the pennant from Willard. 'And this is Desmond, our wicket-keeper, and this . . .' – he waved towards the tallest member of their team, a West Indian boy – '. . . is D. Red-Locks – better known as our demon bowler!'

He then snootily tossed the pennant to Desmond, as if he would get his hands soiled by merely touching it. And Desmond, showing off his wicket-keeping abilities, dived to the side to catch it and then, with a similar look of the fear of contamination, threw it to D. Red-Locks. The West Indian fielded it and tossed it to a fourth boy, who passed it on to the next one, all along the line. Until, eventually, the last boy tossed it to their driver – who wiped his dirty windscreen with it! And that, in the Snobbers' opinion, was all it was good for!

Then Timothy began to swank.

'Our team is coached by a former England player, the super player Jan Booth-Ham.'

'Huh, we're coached by a super player, too. Super Gran!' And Willard pointed proudly to her, standing near by.

But this fib – Super Gran didn't know one end of a

26

cricket bat from the other! – brought forth laughter
from their opponents.

'What?' Timothy exclaimed. 'That old moth-bag?'

'Huh!' she muttered. 'I'll show them.'

She lifted three stumps lying on the pavilion steps
and threw them up in the air. They zoomed down and
plopped into the turf beside each other, as if by magic.
Then she did the same again, with the bails, which
landed smack on target on top of the stumps.

'I'll bet that had you stumped!' she joked, but the
Snobbers, unimpressed, merely sniffed and marched
into the pavilion.

'Come along, James,' Timothy commanded, and
their driver trotted obediently behind them, struggling
with as many of their bats and cricket bags as he could
manage at a time.

'Pooh! Is this where we're expected to change?'
Timothy asked. 'In this grotty little dump?' He
wrinkled his nose with distaste. He wasn't used to
mixing with the lower classes and their broken-down
little buildings.

Presently they emerged from the pavilion in their
whiter-than-white whites. Then D. Red-Locks, their
demon bowler, walked over to a tree, said 'Watch this!'
and demonstrated his prowess as a fast bowler by
bowling a ball at it.

'Huh?' gasped Willard and his team-mates as they
saw the ball splatter into pieces against the trunk!
'Wow! Gulp!'

The Chisleton team shuddered, but they didn't real-

ize it was only a trick ball which was made to shatter on impact. It was a ploy designed to intimidate opponents – and it succeeded! They were intimidated all right!

'It works every time,' Timothy murmured, 'against every team we meet.'

'Yes,' Desmond agreed, 'and gives us an advantage right from the start, what?'

And they laughed.

Rott N. Scoundrel escorted his pupils into town.

'We're here to have a look around,' he explained. 'To case the joint and see if there are any likely crimes worth committing.'

'But – but it's starting to drizzle,' the Scunner moaned. 'And we're all going to get wet.'

'Don't be a baby,' Scoundrel scolded. 'Crooks have got to go out in all kinds of weather.'

They found themselves in a narrow back street, where Scoundrel introduced them to a rear entrance-door which had no fewer than six locks on it.

'Right, lads, lock-picking,' he said. 'Six of you pick a lock – then pick a lock!' He laughed at his own joke while the Scunner, the Muscles, Bill, Wally and Basher all came forward to volunteer.

'You can use anything you've got on your person,' he told them. 'Penknives, bent wire, hairpins . . . Oh no, sorry, that's lady crooks, isn't it?' He looked at the length of the hair on some of the pupils. 'Oh, I don't know, though!' he laughed. 'Or you can even use keys on the locks, if you like!'

But before they got very far in lock-picking, the door was suddenly opened from the other side – and PC Leekie was facing them.

'Now then, now then,' he said. 'What's going on here? What are you lot breaking into the back of the Chisleton nick for, eh?'

'Huh? The back of the nick?' Scoundrel gasped.

'Jings,' said the Scunner, 'I didn't recognize it.'

'No,' Leekie retorted, 'you're more likely to recognize it from the front. You've been in it often enough!'

'Are you implying that we are criminals, officer?' Scoundrel asked, pompously.

'Well these four are for a start, sir,' Leekie replied, pointing to the Scunner and company. 'They're local villains.'

'We've been rumbled, lads,' Scoundrel yelled. 'Scarper!'

They scarpered, they didn't have to be coaxed. And running from the scene of a crime was something they were all experts at!

'You can regard this,' Scoundrel told them, as they ran, 'as a practical lesson in the art of the getaway!'

4 Jobs for the Boys!

Scoundrel and his pupils found themselves in one of Chisleton's back streets, a street full of warehouses, pubs and cafés. He looked over his shoulder, saw they weren't being pursued and told them to slow down.

'Thank . . . puff, puff . . . goodness for that,' the Scunner said. 'I'm out of condition. I'm not cut out for making getaways.'

'You're not cut out to be a crook, either,' Scoundrel retorted.

'What? Humph!' He was hurt and indignant.

'If you ask me,' Scoundrel went on, 'I think you and your men are all pretty incompetent, as crooks.'

The Muscles didn't know what incompetent meant and Cedric took it as a compliment.

'Great!' he said. 'I've never been called incompetent before.'

'Yeah,' added Dustin, grinning inanely, 'and I've never been called pretty before, either.'

Scoundrel pointed towards a nearby pub.

'Come on, lads, I've gotta thirst after all that running. Let's go in for a beer, eh?'

'Yeah,' they agreed, 'and it'll get us in out of the rain.'

'Now,' he said, once they had settled down to enjoy their pints, 'I've got a really practical session for you.'

'And about time, too,' the Scunner muttered.

'You're now,' Scoundrel continued, ignoring him, 'going to get various big jobs to pull. But I'm dividing you into four groups, with each group having a different job to do.'

He wrote the names of the group members on the back of a beer mat. He called Bill and Wally Group A, Windy and Shorty Group B, the Basher brothers Group C and the Scunner and company Group D.

'Group D's got two extra members,' he explained, 'but that's because they're all the one gang. And we're better keeping them all together – they'll do less damage that way!'

'Huh, cheek,' murmured the peeved Scunner as Scoundrel went on:

'Group A can have a go at breaking into someone's safe.'

He looked out of the window at the warehouse across the street, and pointed. 'You might as well make it that one, it's as good as any. Tub, nip across and find out what sort of warehouse it is.'

Tub went, grumbling, and returned to tell them it belonged to Mr L. A. M. Chop, a wholesale and manufacturing butcher.

'Right,' Scoundrel said, marking down on another beer mat that Group A would break into Chop's safe. 'Now, let's see, what's the next job?'

He looked round the pub and spotted a large poster on the wall which advertised: 'THE GREAT CHISLETON PIGEON RACE. The famous

DUCHESS OF OZ from Australia will assist the Mayor in officially starting the race. She will also present the trophy to the winner.'

'That'll do,' he said, pointing. 'Group B can kidnap the race favourite . . .'

'Why don't they kidnap the Duchess while they're at it?' the Scunner sneered, sarcastically.

Scoundrel snapped his fingers. 'Scunner! You're a genius! That's the very thing. One of the groups *can* kidnap her!'

The Scunner sat at the table smirking proudly. So that was *his* group's job? Great. He began to make his acceptance speech!

'I'd just like to say that my men and I will do this job to the best of our ability. You'll be proud of us.'

And then, he thought, Scoundrel would have no cause to call them incompetent again. But he came crashing down to earth when Scoundrel announced:

'*Your* group won't kidnap the Duchess. Group C will do it.'

'What?' the Scunner gasped, unable to believe his ears.

'Yes,' Scoundrel added, 'and Group D will steal the hubcaps off the cars in Chisbury's Department Store car-park, in town.'

Scoundrel went on to add more details to his projects, but the Scunner wasn't listening. What sort of way was that to treat him? He, who had given him the idea in the first place.

But Scoundrel was continuing his instructions:

'When Group C kidnaps the Duchess they'll bring her back to the college and keep her there while they send a ransom note to the mayor – who'll pay a large amount of lolly to have her released. So you'll all be glad I gave you lessons in letter-writing. Right?'

The Bashers nodded. 'We'll do the job all right. No problem.'

Scoundrel continued: 'If she comes by train you could drive my car to Paddleton, board the train, tell her there's a hold-up on the line between there and Chisleton and she's to get off there, but you'll take her the rest of the way by car. It can't fail.'

Then he outlined his plans for the pigeon-snatching and the safe-breaking. And after all that he had about two seconds of advice for the hubcap stealers!

The Scunner had been unusually quiet during all this.

'What's the matter, Uncle?' Tub whispered. 'You all right?'

'Well, in the first place, I can't get my tongue in edgeways! Friend Scoundrel blethers too much! But apart from that I'm speechless! Shocked! Annoyed!'

'What with?' Tub asked.

'I'll tell you what with. Why are all the other groups getting big, prestigious jobs to pull while our group's only getting a wee, insignificant job to do, huh? A job that's beneath our dignity. Stealing hubcaps! I ask you! Huh!'

But Scoundrel overheard him.

'That's the only job your group's fit for, Scunner.

34

But if you do it properly and prove you really are committed crooks then you'll get a bigger, better job to do afterwards.'

'Committed? I'll say we're committed,' the Scunner snorted indignantly. 'We've committed more crimes than you've had fish suppers.'

Scoundrel ignored him and addressed the pupils in general.

'But remember, men, although you've all got your allotted jobs to carry out I want you, at all times, to use your initiative. And I'll award a special diploma to whichever pupil uses his initiative the most during the next few days.'

As Edison arrived at Chisleton Park to watch the cricket match, the rain became heavier and heavier. She was surprised to see Muggins, Leekie and some of their colleagues there, until she remembered their connection with the Boys' Club; they were there to cheer the lads on.

The rain continued as one of the umpires, Mr Bowler, approached Willard and Timothy Toff, the two captains, with a bat, for the 'toss up'. But Timothy took one look at the bat and refused to use it.

'What? That old thing?' he snorted. 'You *must* be joking! It's old and cracked and dirty and tatty.' He turned to Desmond. 'Dessy, give me *my* bat, will you, old man!'

'Certainly, Timmers,' Desmond replied, and handed his captain a bat with a handle inlaid with gold leaf.

36

'Yes, that's better,' Toff said. 'That's more like a cricket bat. Right, shall I call?'

The umpire spun the bat. Timothy won the toss and decided the Snobbers would bowl.

'Off you go and pad up,' he ordered Willard. 'That is, if you've *got* pads!' He looked around at the park, the cricket area and the pavilion. 'You probably haven't, in a dump-heap like this.'

'We *have*,' Willard snorted angrily, as he and his opening partner indignantly shuffled up the pavilion steps to put their leg-guards on.

They emerged, minutes later, all too aware that the pads, like the rest of their equipment, were tatty and grubby compared to the Snobbers' first-class items.

'Remind us to let you have our old gear when we're finished with it,' Timothy sneered as they reached the wicket. 'We get new gear each season, of course.'

'You *would*,' Willard muttered.

'Naturally,' Timothy boasted, 'with us having wealthy parents, don't ya know.'

Willard ignored him and took his stance at the wicket.

Timothy arranged his fielders in a tight circle around Willard, so that he had the distinct feeling there were ten ogres breathing fire at him from very close range, daring him to breathe, let alone hit the ball when it was bowled at him. Not that he had much chance when the ball *was* bowled.

He took guard and then, quaking in his cricket boots, he saw the massive figure of D. Red-Locks pacing back to start his huge run-up to the wicket. Then he took one look at the demon bowler as he came thundering back on his run and that was enough for him. Remembering the splattered ball on the tree trunk he couldn't help himself – he closed his eyes as the ball was bowled.

It pitched towards him, hit the ground, bounced – and the only sounds he heard were the click as his middle stump went flying off somewhere behind him and Red-Locks' cry of 'Howzat?'

'Out!' said the umpire, and Willard was trudging back to the pavilion, more despondent than ever.

'Quack, quack!' Timothy jeered, as Willard walked past him.

Then the others took up the 'duck' calls, making him blush furiously. And, as he passed Red-Locks, the bowler made as if to bowl a ball at his head, yelling 'Duck!' at him!

The next man in fared no better and was also out for a duck; as was the next, and the next.

'Nothing but ducks,' Willard moaned, from where he now sat on the pavilion steps.

'And it looks as if it's going to be the weather for ducks as well,' Edison said ruefully.

She was sitting with Super Gran and she put her hand up and found that it was now raining fairly hard.

'Maybe rain'll stop play,' Super Gran suggested.

'It would be better just playing on,' Willard said. 'We might as well get it over and done with. Otherwise we'll just have to have a replay and I don't think I could face all this again.'

5 It's Not Cricket!

The rain at the cricket match worsened, until it became torrential.

'Umpire, you'll have to call a halt,' Timothy Toff protested. 'My whites are being ruined.'

'You'll need to get covers out and protect this wicket,' Desmond added.

'What covers?' Mr Bowler asked. 'This is Chisleton Public Park, it's not the posh Snobbers' Club, you know.'

'Such insolence,' Toff said, as they ran towards the pavilion for shelter. 'I shall report you for that, umpire.'

'Oh, go jump in the lake,' Mr Bowler said, fed up to the teeth with the little – huge! – twerps.

The weather didn't improve, and for the next hour the dismal Chisleton team sat in the pavilion looking out at the deluge, with Super Gran and Edison, while the Snobbers made a lot of noise as they boasted of how great their team was and how they had beaten every other team in the league for years.

The rain drove the spectators away, there being no point in sitting around indefinitely in the open, getting soaked, in the hope that the weather would improve.

'Look, little man,' Timothy addressed Mr Bowler,

'it's about time you declared that rain has stopped play. The pitch is unplayable. That is, it's even more unplayable than it was when we arrived. Really, it's one of the worst . . .'

'All right,' Mr Bowler cut in, to stop Timothy's moans. 'But the match will have to be replayed within two days.'

'Oh! Groans! Will it?' sighed Willard, hoping that that could have been an end to it.

'Maybe we won't have to replay the match,' said his pal, who was dreading it. 'Maybe something'll happen, eh? Maybe the world'll end!'

Even the Snobbers weren't pleased at the news of the replay. They thought they'd be awarded the match points without having to return to Chisleton. After all, the Chisleton innings was almost over – and they had yet to score!

'Oh, I say, a replay?' Timothy pouted. 'But that means having to travel all the way from Poshtown again!'

And Poshtown was all of twelve miles away!

They sent their driver out into the rain to bring the minibus to the pavilion steps, so they wouldn't get any wetter as they climbed aboard it.

'Hey, you can't bring it across the grass,' Mr Bowler yelled, then decided to say no more. They'd only report him to their rich fathers, who'd get Chisleton thrown out of the league altogether.

'Good riddance to them,' he muttered, as the Snobbers piled into their minibus and it sped off towards Poshtown.

'Yeah, we all say that,' Willard agreed. 'But do we really *have* to replay them, Mr Bowler?'

'I'm afraid so, it's the league rules.'

Willard and his team-mates were more depressed than ever.

But next day, when it was dry, Super Gran persuaded the boys to go to Chisleton Common for a practice session.

'What's the point, Gran?' Willard asked. 'If they're going to clobber us they're going to clobber us. We don't need to practise just to be clobbered!'

But she managed to coax them and, after studying one of his cricket books – to try to understand the game! – she offered to give them some coaching.

But it took her some time to get used to the terms!

'You,' she instructed one of the boys, 'stand out there at silly midden.'

'You mean silly mid-on, Super Gran,' he corrected her.

'Aye, something like that. And you, Willard, try bowling a boogie.'

'D'you not mean a googly, Gran?'

'Aye, you're right. Och, I'll never get used to these maidens over in the gully in their slips,' she laughed.

She herself did some bowling – but not quite at Super-speed! – to give the batsmen a chance to see what it was like to face up to D. Red-Locks, so that when they faced him again they would be more prepared, and wouldn't all be bowled out for a duck.

41

'It won't make much difference, Gran,' Willard insisted. 'We *still* won't beat 'em.'

'No, but at least you can try to put up more of a show next time. In fact, if *you* manage to keep your eyes open it'll be an improvement on last time!'

The rearranged match was due to take place on the same day as the Chisleton Pigeon Race. Mr Bowler, the umpire, who was also the match secretary, had forgotten about that, so any spectator who wanted to see both events would have to choose one or the other – or dash about between them! And the match, this time, would be played at the local Cricket Club's ground, as the pitch in the park was completely waterlogged.

Super Gran was quite looking forward to the match, especially now that she knew a little bit more about the game! But Willard and his team-mates were still dreading it; having already encountered the Snobbers, they didn't relish meeting them again.

The Scunner banged the billiard table, causing Dustin, who was playing snooker, to rip the green baize cloth with his cue. But the Scunner didn't notice, he was too busy complaining about Scoundrel and his Crooks' College.

'Who does he think he is, saying my gang aren't proper crooks! Saying we're incompetent. Cheek! And what's he teaching us, anyway? Not a lot. It'll take years for me to become the world's greatest crook at this rate. And especially if we're not allowed to do anything except pinch hubcaps. Huh, that was the last straw!'

'Why *do* thieves pinch hubcaps, Uncle?' Tub asked.

'I dunno.'

And the Muscles, when Tub asked them, didn't know either. It was something which had always puzzled them, too.

'Right, lads,' he said, resolutely, 'enough is enough. I'm going to show that rotten Rott N. Scoundrel just what we can do.'

'What *can* we do?' Cedric asked him.

'We can outwit all those other pupils, that's what.'

'Can we?' Dustin was amazed. 'How?'

'We can do it, Muscles, if we *muscle* in on those other groups. If we pull the jobs they're going to pull – before they pull 'em!'

'Wot for?' Tub asked.

'' Cos that way I'll get my diploma from the college for passing the course – the first rung on the ladder to success. And besides, if I nobble those other groups, that's using my initiative, isn't it? And I'd get the special diploma for that, too. And that would show Scoundrel if we're incompetent or not.'

'But what do we have to do?' Tub asked.

'Well, to begin with, Dustin can rob the butcher's safe, before Bill and Wally do it.'

'But I didn't understand all that about dials and tumblers,' Dustin admitted with a frown, referring to Scoundrel's lesson.

'Don't worry,' the Scunner said, 'you won't have to break into the safe, you'll have the keys.'

'Oh, that's OK then.' The frown on Dustin, safe-breaker, broke into its silly grin again.

'And when Windy and Shorty nick the Pigeon Race favourite – Tub will nick it back again. Then I'll return it to Scoundrel, to show that *our* group is cleverer than Windy's group.'

'And do I kidnap the Duchess of Oz?' Cedric asked.

'That's right.'

'And what are you going to do, Uncle?' Tub asked. 'While we're all doing these jobs? Huh?'

'I, Tub, have already done my bit – thinking up all these plans which you three are going to put into operation. See?'

'Humph,' Tub grumbled, 'that was the easy part.'

'Aye, but you didn't think of it, did you, Tub? And I did. And that's why I'm the boss of this gang and you're just one of my minions, or, as we say in Glasgow – mini yins!'

Dustin was wearing his worried frown again.

'How do I get the safe key, Boss?' he asked.

'The best way's to do it as an inside job,' the Scunner said. 'Hold on a minute.'

He looked in the phone directory, found L. A. M. Chop's number and then lifted the phone and dialled.

'Hello, this is your local V A T office. We're sending Dustin . . . er . . . our *Mr* Dustin to inspect your V A T books. He'll be along this morning. Goodbye.

'There you are, that's got you into his office. So now you can find out where the safe keys are kept.'

45

'What? A job? You mean – work?' He was shattered by the suggestion.

'He's never worked in his life,' Cedric explained. 'Not since he was expelled from school at six!'

'Don't worry, you won't be there long,' the Scunner said.

He brought a city businessman's suit and bowler hat out of his wardrobe and got Dustin to put them on. Then he handed him a briefcase and rolled umbrella.

'I look a right twit,' Dustin said, looking in the mirror.

'Aye, but no one'll suspect you. *All* VAT inspectors dress like that. Oh, and if he doesn't believe you know anything about business and you want to impress him, just rattle off some things about Stocks and Shares.'

'Huh?' said Dustin, stupidly. 'But I don't know anything about socks and stares, I mean Stocks and Shares.'

'Well, if you say this to him he'll think you know what you're talking about. Listen . . .'

And the Scunner recited a long rigmarole of non-sensical bits and pieces of financial talk, which was utterly meaningless.

Presently, Dustin was being ushered into an old-fashioned office where Chop sat at an old-fashioned desk. He rose to shake his hand.

'Ah, Mr . . . er . . . Dustbin from the VAT office?'

He thought: 'Dustbin? That's a strange name!'

But out loud he said: 'What can I do for you?'

'You can let me see your safe!'

46

'What? My safe?'

'Er . . . no . . . um . . . I mean . . . I'll need to get all your . . . um . . . financial papers and VAT books out of your safe.'

'Oh yes, yes of course you will,' Chop agreed. 'Follow me.'

6   A Safe Safe –
and a Pop Pianist!

Mr Chop led Dustin from his office, through the reception area where his secretary worked and into the meat factory itself. But Dustin, as they reached the far end of it, thought Chop had rumbled him and was throwing him out. So, to prevent this happening, he quoted the Scunner's Stocks and Shares nonsense at the man.

'I know all about fi-fi-financial matters, Mr Chop. The Sock Exchange. Er ... I mean ... the Stock Exchange. Shocks and scares ... um ... no, I mean ... socks and spares ... no, I mean ... Stocks and Shares. Sell Debenture Bonds and Ernie Bonds, and buy James Bond's. Sell blue chips, buy fish 'n' chips. Invest in guilty secure ET's. Or should that be gilt-edge securities? Invest in silver and steel. Or is it – steal silver vests? Oh ... um ... ah ...'

The Scunner's nonsense was even more nonsensical now that Dustin had put his own interpretation on it.

But as he spouted forth this gibberish Mr Chop whipped a pen and notepad out of his pocket and scribbled away like mad. Then he said 'Excuse me', dashed to the nearest phone extension, spoke excitedly for a few seconds, calmed down, replaced the receiver

and rejoined Dustin, who stood with his mouth wide open, puzzled.

'Ah, now here's the meat safe,' he said, 'this is what you want.' And he took Dustin over to a large door at one side of the building. 'Or the cold store, as we call it.'

'Huh?' said Dustin. 'But-but I meant your office safe, where you keep your "bread" – not the one where you keep your meat!'

'Oh, but I've been very clever about that,' Chop said proudly. 'I keep it in here. It's so cold that no one could stay long enough to rob it. Good idea, eh?'

He opened the store's heavy security door and led the way through the cold vapour and past the frozen carcasses of cows, sheep and pigs which hung from the hooks in the ceiling.

'Huh? It's in here?' Dustin said, waving the mist aside as he tried to locate it.

Chop led him into the far corner of the room where the large, frost-encrusted safe was situated. Then he produced his key-ring and opened its door.

Dustin reckoned he'd have to tell the Scunner about this right away, in case Bill and Wally got to it before them.

'Here you are,' said Chop, ignoring the money and lifting his VAT books out, to hand them to Dustin.

'Huh? Wot are these?' Dustin asked.

'They're what you asked for, my VAT books.'

'Oh, yeah, yeah, I forgot about them!'

Chop locked the safe and they left the cold store,

closing the door behind them. Dustin was all for walking out of the factory's back door, to report to the Scunner waiting outside, but Chop led him to the office again.

Dustin sat at a desk and 'worked' for a little while, not knowing what he was expected to work at! And not knowing a VAT book from a vat of cheese!

But presently Chop left the office to visit the factory again so Dustin, knowing he wouldn't be missed, sneaked out to report to the Scunner about the problem of the cold store.

But the Scunner wasn't stuck for long. Glancing round the street he spotted, amongst the pubs, cafés and warehouses, a shop nearby which sold camping equipment. He led his men across to it, saw an outfit in the window which an Arctic explorer would be happy to wear as he sought the North Pole, and went in to hire it.

'This is the very thing to get you into the cold store long enough to rob the safe.'

'Yeah,' Dustin agreed.

The Scunner handed him the parcelled outfit.

'Smuggle it into the office and hide it till you can get the safe key.'

'OK, Boss.'

Newcastle Brown, the famous pop pianist and singer, was speeding along the Chisleton ring road towards town in his silver Poshe car. Sitting beside him in the front seat was Bony Part, a crook, while Clyde, Bony's

51

assistant, sat on the back seat with a basket on his knees.

'I hope the Lass will be all right, Bony.'

But it wasn't a wife or girlfriend Newcastle was talking about.

'Is she all right in there?' he asked Clyde, over his shoulder.

But it wasn't a little daughter who was crammed into the small hamper – it was his pigeon, whose full name was Fast Lass!

And she was fast all right. In fact, she was the favourite to win the great Chisleton Pigeon Race this year, and Newcastle and company were taking her there to take part in the race.

'Clyde,' Bony said, turning in his seat to address him. 'CLYDE!' he shouted. 'Newcastle's asking if . . .'

But Clyde didn't hear him. He was wearing headphones and was listening, blissfully, with his eyes closed, to his favourite tape on his personal stereo. But he wasn't listening to Newcastle's kind of music, pop music, he was listening to the opera *Carmen*. For the crooked Clyde was a ballet and opera lover!

'Yeah, she'll be all right,' Bony told Newcastle as he turned to face the front again, still not having caught Clyde's attention. 'And she'll win.'

'But apart from the prize,' Newcastle said, 'I've got a big bet on, so I stand to gain a large amount of cash. Oh, and did you find a minder? I asked you to get someone in Chisleton to look after the Lass till after the race.'

'I'm working on it,' Bony said, as the Poshe sped towards town.

'And remember, I'm due to play those gigs in Chisleton while the race is on. *And* before that. So *I* can't look after her. And you and Clyde know nothing about birds, do you?'

'Not that type, no!' said Bony.

Newcastle turned in his seat again, to ask Clyde:

'Hey, talking of gigs, did you remember to load my portable electronic piano, Clyde?'

But Clyde still didn't hear him and he still had his eyes closed as he beat time to the *Toreador Song*.

'Don't worry,' Bony said, answering for him. 'It's on the roof-rack.'

'And my luggage?'

'In the boot.'

'And the Lass's corn and greens and . . .'

'Beside your luggage.'

'You're not forgetting the pigeon minder?' Newcastle asked again, as the car approached Chisleton.

'Stop worrying, will you?'

Bony had been thinking of someone who would be suitable as a minder and had decided to approach the Scunner, not because he was suitable but because he owed Bony a favour. And besides, he didn't know anyone else in Chisleton and he'd be quicker getting him than trying to find someone else.

'I don't care who you get,' Newcastle said, 'as long as he's reliable.'

Well, Bony thought, that lets the Scunner out! But,

after all, it was only for a couple of days and what could go wrong in that time? And besides, he and Clyde would be there to keep their eye on him.

As they drove into the town centre they saw the flags and bunting hanging from the trees and lampposts and the general air of festivity which the annual Pigeon Race brought to the place. And they even saw one of the local postmen, Postman Pugh, delivering his mail like a uniformed Long John Silver – with a stuffed pigeon attached to his shoulder!

They stopped at a hotel and booked rooms for a couple of nights. Then, while Bony went off to phone the Scunner, Newcastle entertained the customers in the lounge bar with his portable piano.

'Hello, Scunner, this is Bony – Bony and Clyde. We're in town with Newcastle Brown, the pop pianist. We've got a job for you.'

'Hold on, Bony,' the Scunner said, 'there's something wrong with the phone. It's full of rotten clanking noises . . .'

'That's not the phone,' Bony laughed, 'that's Newcastle playing his hit tunes to the punters in the lounge. It's his electronic piano.'

'Ooyah! Ow-ow-ow!' Newcastle suddenly shrieked, in pain.

'Sorry about that,' Bony apologized. 'It was just Clyde – he's a music lover, you see.'

'No, I don't see. And what was he yelling at?'

'Oh, *he* wasn't yelling, it was Newcastle. Clyde walked past his piano and slammed the lid down on his fingers, accidentally – on purpose!'

'Oof, nasty,' the Scunner sympathized.

'It could've been worse,' Bony said. 'It could've been a real piano, with a heavy lid.'

'Oops, sorry,' Clyde apologized, but didn't mean a word of it!

'Anyway,' Bony continued, 'Newcastle wants you to act as his minder for a couple of days.'

'Minder, eh?' said the Scunner. 'Aye, righto.'

'We're coming over to your house to discuss it with you,' Bony said, ringing off.

7 Pigeon Minder

When Newcastle and company arrived at the Scunner's villa the Scunner toadied up to the pop star, thinking that, as Newcastle was famous, this was the thing to do.

'May I call you Newcastle, Newcastle?' the Scunner asked.

'No, 'cos my name isn't Newcastle Newcastle, it's Newcastle Brown!' he laughed.

'Aye, right. Very droll. So may I call you Newcastle?' he went on, smiling expectantly.

'You may call me "sir",' Newcastle said, loftily.

'Right. Yes, sir, whatever you say, sir. Certainly. Yes.' The Scunner grovelled happily.

'Newcastle's got something for you,' Bony said.

'Oh, you shouldn't have bothered.' The Scunner thought it was a present!

'Something for you to mind for him,' Bony continued.

'Anything. Anything at all,' he fawned. 'It would give me considerable pleasure to ...'

'To belt up!' interrupted Clyde, who was getting fed up with the Scunner's grovelling.

'Right. Right,' he said, adding: 'Is there ... is there any payment for minding whatever it is I'll be minding?'

Newcastle lifted his pigeon basket off the floor and placed it on the table, but the Scunner didn't recognize what it was.

'Is this the payment?' He sounded disappointed. 'Is it one of those food hampers full of the rubbish that rich folk eat?'

'Like caviar and dead peasants?' said Dustin.

'Not peasants, peasant! Pheasants,' the Scunner corrected him.

But Cedric, who knew a bit about pigeons, recognized a pigeon basket.

'Boss, it's a . . .' he began, but Newcastle forestalled him by opening it and proudly showing them his champion racer.

The Scunner, who knew nothing about pigeons, wasn't impressed. He didn't know that this was the race favourite, but even if he had known he still wouldn't have been impressed.

'Newcastle wants you to keep your eye on it,' Bony explained, 'from now until after the race. *He'll* be too busy playing a concert while the race's on.'

'It's not an "it", it's a "she",' Newcastle corrected, indignantly. 'Her name's Fast Lass. And a pop concert's a "gig". And this is an open-air gig, in Chisleton Park.'

'Oh, you're playing al fresco?' the Scunner said, showing off his little bit of knowledge.

'Al Fresco?' said the puzzled Newcastle. 'No, Al's not playing with me, it's a solo gig. And who's Al? I've never heard of him. What does he play – guitar?'

58

'Listen,' Bony said, 'I heard in the hotel bar that some rotten scoundrel by the name of Rott N. Scoundrel intends getting his hoodlums to pinch the race favourite.'

'Gulp! Is that so?' the Scunner said, innocently.

'And that's Fast Lass, here, so you'll have to guard it . . .'

'"Her",' Newcastle corrected, 'not "it".'

'OK, her. You'll have to guard her with your life.'

'Have you *heard* of Scoundrel?' Newcastle asked, suspiciously.

'Gulp! No, not really,' the Scunner lied.

'Hey, Boss, you *have* heard of Scoun . . .' Dustin began, but the Scunner kicked him on the shin, under the table. 'Ouch!'

'I *have* heard of scoundrels, certainly,' he said, blushing, 'but not of Rott N. Scoundrel.'

He hoped they wouldn't connect the blush with the fib.

'But Boss . . .' Dustin began again, adding: 'Ooyah!' as his other shin was suddenly kicked by Cedric.

'Fast Lass,' Bony explained, 'isn't just the favourite, she's the hottest favourite to win in years.'

'And besides that,' Newcastle added, 'I've got a large bet on and I stand to win a small fortune. So I don't want anything, or anyone, getting in the way of it. Understand?'

'Yeah, understand?' Clyde repeated, threateningly.

He thumped his fist into his palm with a resounding smack, which promised what would happen to the

Scunner if Fast Lass didn't win the race. And as Clyde was a large man with knuckles like an earthmover's bucket the Scunner thought it best if he did as he was told. Especially when his face got a close encounter with them, as a hint that any disobedience on *his* part would result in his denting those knuckles with his chin!

'Gulp! OK, so I look after the pigeon – but I don't know anything about pigeons!'

Bony whipped out a wad of banknotes and waved them at him.

'Maybe these will help you to learn?'

He peeled a few off and handed them over. 'Here's some meantime, for expenses. To rent a loft, and whatever you need . . .'

'A loft?' the puzzled Scunner interrupted. 'You mean – someone's attic?'

'No, a pigeon loft,' Newcastle said, scornfully. 'But you won't need any feeding stuff, there's plenty in the basket.'

The three men left the Scunner's house and, on the way out, Newcastle presented him with a large cigar.

'Here, keep it till after the race. You can smoke it to celebrate Fast Lass's win. And the big win I'll make on my bet.'

'Thanks, Newcastle . . . er . . . Mr Brown, sir,' the Scunner said as he stuck the cigar into his jacket pocket.

But after Bony and company had left Tub looked worried.

60

'What are you going to do about this, Uncle?' he asked.

'We'll just have to learn all about pigeons, I suppose.'

'*I* know a bit about pigeons, Boss,' Cedric said, eagerly.

'No, I didn't mean that,' Tub explained. 'I meant – how are we going to stop Windy and Shorty from pinching Fast Lass for Scoundrel's project? Huh?'

'Aye,' the Scunner said, 'I forgot we were going to let them pinch the favourite and then steal it away from them. Aye, that *is* a problem, isn't it? I'll have to think about it.'

Postman Pugh stood on the path outside his pigeon loft in the allotment gardens, stroking his pigeon – his real live one this time, as opposed to the stuffed one he carried on his postal rounds.

'Hello, Pughie,' Super Gran greeted him as she and the children approached the loft. 'What's your bird called?'

'Rosy Redlips.'

'Is she called after your wife?' Edison asked.

'What? Called after *her*?' Pugh was horrified. 'She's dead annoyed at all the time I spend with Rosy. If I called the bird after my wife I'd have to call her "Jealous Janet"!'

'Pugh!' screeched a voice in the near distance.

'Oh-oh!' he murmured. 'Speak of the devil! Or rather, the she-devil! Here she is, now!'

Janet came striding up the path towards them, brandishing a rolling-pin.

'Here you are again. You're always here. Always spending your time with that dratted bird. You spend more time with it than you do with me . . .'

'It's not an "it", it's a "she",' Pugh interrupted, but she ignored him and continued her tirade:

'You never take *me* anywhere, oh, no, but you're always taking that bird places. Races and shows and things . . .'

'Yak, yak, yak . . .' muttered Pugh.

'What was that?'

'Nothing,' he sighed, as he stroked Rosy Redlips again.

Super Gran gestured for Willard and Edison to follow her as she walked away from the loft.

'We don't want to get involved in a family feud,' she said with a smile.

They continued along the path and passed a few more pigeon lofts, until Willard pointed.

'Look, there's the Scunner.'

'I didn't know *he* was a pigeon fancier,' Edison said.

He was standing outside one of the lofts and was holding Fast Lass in his hand, nervously, at arm's length, as if he didn't quite know what to do with her. Tub and Dustin stood around, looking equally nervous, while Cedric was emerging from the loft.

'I'm surprised, Scunner,' Super Gran greeted him when they reached his rented loft. 'I never knew you were a pigeon fancier.'

'I'm not! I don't fancy pigeons at all. I'm just looking after it for a friend.'

'What's its name?' she asked.

'How should I know? I didn't know they *had* names.'

'It's called Last Grass,' Dustin told them, grinning his normal – stupid! – grin, and added: 'Maybe it's called after a police informant, eh? Grass – get it?'

'No, it's called Past Glass,' Tub claimed, probably thinking of a drink of Coke he'd recently had!

'You're both wrong, it's Fast Lass,' Cedric said, remembering what Newcastle had told them.

Postman Pugh, his stuffed pigeon back on his shoulder, his pigeon-jealous wife having departed in a huff, approached them and recognized the name.

'Fast Lass?' he exclaimed. 'That's Newcastle Brown's bird, isn't it? The race favourite?'

'What? Newcastle Brown?' Willard and Edison cried, in unison. 'The pop pianist?'

They were thrilled to bits to think that the famous pop star was in the neighbourhood.

'He's playing a pop concert in the park while the race is on,' explained the Scunner, still glancing nervously at the pigeon in his hand, in case she bit him. 'Al fresco.'

'Who's Al?' Willard asked. 'I've never heard of him.'

'Does he play the guitar?' Edison asked.

'Oh, don't start that again,' he muttered, as he took Fast Lass into the loft.

8   A Lookalike for a Lass

Later, the Scunner and company were watching Fast Lass peck at a tin of corn.

'Cedric,' he said, 'as you seem to know all about pigeons you can look after it.'

'Not "it", "her",' Tub corrected.

The Scunner ignored him and continued, to Cedric:

'And do it properly. There's a big fat fee for us after the race, from Newcastle. From his winnings *and* his bet.'

'Yeah, OK,' Cedric said. 'But see what I've got.' He whipped a newspaper out of his pocket. 'It's the *Pij Post*, for fanciers. It's all about pigeons, see?'

'Well done, Ceddie,' the Scunner said. 'Did you buy it?'

'You're joking! I nicked it outa Chisleton news-agent's! And look . . .' He pointed to a picture of Fast Lass on the front page.

'Yeah, but what are we going to do about Windy and Shorty pinching her?' Tub asked again. It was clearly worrying him.

'I've given it some thought,' the Scunner said. 'Each of us could take it in turns to guard the loft all night, to prevent them, couldn't we?'

'But what if one of us falls asleep on guard and

doesn't notice what's going on, and they steal her anyway?' Tub asked.

'OK,' his uncle said, 'then two of us will stand guard together, each time. First you and me, then the Muscles.'

But Tub still frowned worriedly.

'But what if *they* both fall asleep, Uncle,' he persisted, 'or *we* both fall asleep?'

'Aye, that's possible,' the Scunner agreed.

He gave it some more thought, then snapped his fingers.

'We'll move Fast Lass to another loft, a "safe house", and substitute another pigeon that looks like her. Then, if they steal the bird they'll steal the wrong one and Fast Lass will be safe elsewhere. Good, eh?'

'Yeah, that's a good idea, Uncle,' Tub said, happy at last.

'But where do we get a substitute pigeon?' Cedric asked.

'Och, any old bird'll do as a lookalike,' the Scunner said. 'All pigeons look the same!'

'They don't, Boss,' Cedric argued, pulling out his *Pij Post* and pointing to the various birds in it, showing him that they didn't look alike. 'They've all got different colours and markings. See?'

'OK, OK,' he said. 'So we'll have to beg, buy, borrow or steal a lookalike pigeon from somewhere. Right?'

So the search was on for a Fast Lass lookalike, and the Scunner and Muscles spent the next few hours breaking into all the pigeon lofts in town to have a look at the residents. Eventually they found one with Fast Lass's colours and markings, but they had to buy it from her owner. Her name was Slow Flo.

Tub wasn't with the others when they bought her and, not knowing they'd got one, he was still on the look-out for a lookalike pigeon. And he found one!

Rott N. Scoundrel had given his pupils an assignment to carry out that day.

'I want you to choose someone at random to follow,' he had said. 'You don't have to follow them far, maybe just for a few miles, but don't let them spot you. Go to it, lads.'

'Huh, we haven't time for all that nonsense,' the Scunner had said. 'We're too busy looking for a look-alike pigeon to bother with Scoundrel and his daft assignments.'

'But if we don't do it,' Tub pointed out, 'you won't complete the course and won't get your diploma.'

'Aye, that's true,' his uncle agreed. 'Tell you what, *you* do it for us. After all, we don't *all* have to do it, do we?'

So Tub had been delegated to do the 'following' project.

But after strolling aimlessly around the High Street for some time without seeing anyone worth following, he became peckish and, as he was passing Chisleton's large Department Store, Chisbury's, he decided to pop into their food hall.

His eye was caught by a large chocolate gateau in

one of the freezers. But as he lifted it out his eye was caught by something in the freezer's delicatessen compartment. It was an exact replica of Fast Lass, with the identical colours and markings. It was a frozen pigeon, of course, but that couldn't be helped.

After checking that no one was watching, he whipped it out of the freezer and thrust it inside his jacket – beside the already whipped gateau, topped with whipped cream! Then he casually strolled out of the store again, smuggling the stolen goods past the check-out women.

Outside, he pulled the pigeon out of his jacket and looked at it. 'I'm gonna call you Chisbury, after the store!'

He put it into his jacket pocket and then, looking up, he spotted Super Gran and company in the distance and realized he'd found his assignment 'victims'.

'Goody, they'll do. I'll follow them,' he murmured.

Then, happily munching his way through the chocolate gateau, he followed them from the High Street to Chisleton Common.

'I wonder what they're doing here?' he said as he saw them meeting Inventor Black.

He hid behind a tree and watched, as Black said:

'I wanted to demonstrate my latest, greatest invention.'

'Yes, but why up here, Blackie?' Super Gran asked.

'Because I need lots of space to demonstrate it.'

'Why?' asked Willard.

'I'll show you,' he replied, taking a small object out

68

of his pocket. 'Actually I've got two new inventions to show you. This is the first one.'

'What is it?' Edison asked.

'It's a mini, rocket-powered catapult, which is extremely powerful and far-reaching for its size. It can shoot objects a terrific distance and that's why I need lots of space here on the Common to try it out.'

'So let's see it, then,' Super Gran said.

'Right, watch this,' he said.

He switched it on, loaded a golf ball, which he'd brought for the purpose, and fired it. And the onlookers had trouble keeping their eyes on it as it zoomed out of sight across the Common.

'Now you see why I'm demonstrating it here. Anything fired from it goes such a distance that I couldn't have tried it out in the centre of town. I might've hit someone – miles away!'

'It's landed in the Chisle Pond,' said Super Gran, who had managed to follow the ball's flight with her Super-vision. 'Jings, that's some distance! Your mini catapult's a Super-catapult!'

'Wow!' said Willard, impressed.

'And I've got such confidence in it,' Black said, 'that I hope to go into business, selling them. I've already made about a dozen of them, all ready to sell to the shops.'

'What's your other gadget, Blackie?' Super Gran asked.

'This,' he said, taking a small metal object out of his pocket. 'It's a "silent" flute for animals.'

70

'But dogs already have silent *whistles*,' Willard pointed out.

'Yes,' he agreed, 'but not ones that play nice little *tunes* for the nice little doggies.'

'You mean,' said Edison with a smile, 'ones like "How much is that doggie in the window"?'

Black blew it and all five of them, including Tub from behind his tree, watched as a nearby sparrow came swooping down and fluttered around their heads, as if dancing in mid-air.

'See,' said Black, 'he's enjoying the tune.'

'What was it this time,' Edison asked, laughing, '"Sparrow in the tree top"?'

'Isn't this something like that gadget you invented for the Pigeon Race?' Super Gran asked.

She was referring to a remote-controlled radio implement for making the pigeons fly in a huge circle, starting and finishing at Chisleton, instead of the normal pigeon race, where pigeons fly between two points, from A to B.

'Yes,' Black agreed, 'it's similar.'

Tub had to remain behind the tree until they left to return to town, and then he was able to follow them.

He looked forward to returning to his uncle's house to show him Chisbury, the perfect lookalike for Fast Lass, and tell him about Black's new gadgets. But he was annoyed when his uncle and the Muscles merely laughed at him.

'Don't be silly, Tub, how can a frozen pigeon possibly

be used as a substitute for a real live one?' the Scunner said.

'But it's just something for Windy and Shorty to grab in the dark,' Tub pointed out. 'It doesn't matter if it's alive, or not.'

'Well anyway,' he was told, 'we've already got a lookalike pigeon. Slow Flo is her name and she *is* a live one! So we don't need your rotten old frozen one, see?'

'Humph!' Tub mumbled. 'How was I to know you had one? I did my best, didn't I?'

9 A Dumpling – and a Decoy!

That morning at the Police Station, an excited, nervous young PC Dumpling, dressed in his spotless new uniform, was joining the Chisleton force as a recruit.

'Hello, good morning and welcome,' Muggins greeted him.

'Hello, good morning – and thank you, sir,' he replied.

Dumpling was given his badges of office – his notebook and pen, personal radio, truncheon, handcuffs and special helmet. This was one with a revolving blue light on top and a police siren which went 'Ee-aw, ee-aw, ee-aw' when its wearer was in pursuit of a criminal!

'You just press this button here,' P C Leekie instructed Dumpling as he tried it on for size.

'Now,' said Muggins, 'it's time for your first foot-patrol. You've got all your gear, so good luck. But remember, you're only here for a trial period to begin with, to see if you can do the work and fit in with the Chisleton Constabulary.'

'Yes, sir, thank you, sir,' P C Dumpling replied, nervously.

But in his excitement he tripped down the station

steps, fell headlong into the street and Leekie and another constable, PC Peasea, had to rush out and lift him up.

'That's the first time I've ever been picked up by the police,' Dumpling giggled nervously.

As he strolled round the town on patrol, he put his hand up to scratch his ear and pressed his helmet button by mistake, setting off its siren and giving everyone in sight a nervous breakdown as they leapt for their lives! And his traffic duty resulted in a complete pile-up of cars honking at him, making him panic and run round in circles trying to sort it all out.

'Good grief!' Leekie muttered, when he saw this and hurried to help. 'No wonder he was called Dumbo Dumpling at Police College!'

The traffic snarl-up was finally cleared and Leekie walked Dumpling back to the station, wondering if perhaps the recruit was not cut out to be a policeman.

'Go and dust out cell No. 1,' Leekie told him – but Dumpling somehow managed to get himself locked in while doing so!

'You can do some desk duty,' said Muggins, thinking that this would keep the recruit out of trouble.

It did – until one of the phones rang.

'Hello?' Dumpling answered it.

But then the other phones on the desk also began ringing furiously – all nine of them!

'Hello . . . hello . . . hello . . . hello . . . hello . . .' he said, grabbing each of them in turn and trying his best to answer them all.

But he was all confused, and got himself tied up in their cords and cables, which twisted round him.

'Oh dear, oh dear,' moaned Muggins, shaking his head in despair. But Dumpling remained cheerful.

'Don't worry, Boss . . .'

'Don't call me Boss!' Muggins screamed at him.

'OK. But don't worry, Spec . . .'

'And don't call me Spec, either!' Muggins interrupted.

'OK, but don't worry, I'll soon get the hang of it. Honestly.'

'You'd better,' Muggins screeched. 'Or else you'll hand in your truncheon, handcuffs and radio, and you'll resign.'

'Oh no!' said the keen recruit, going pale.

'Oh yes!' retorted Muggins as he left Dumpling to it, still struggling with the cords and cables which entangled him.

'Hello . . . hello . . . hello . . .' he continued at the ten phones, wondering if he should ever have entered the police force in the first place.

That night the Scunner's plan was put into operation. They smuggled Fast Lass out of her loft in the allotments and took her to the 'safe house' loft they had found at the other end of town. Then they returned to the first loft and took turns, in pairs, to keep watch, to fool Windy and Shorty when they came along to steal Newcastle's pigeon.

'Maybe they won't come after all,' Tub said, as he

and the Scunner headed for the loft, to relieve the Muscles on guard duty.

'They will. The race is tomorrow, so they'll have to pinch the pigeon tonight.'

But ahead of them, at the allotments, Windy and Shorty were creeping stealthily up the path and when they reached the loft they spotted the Muscles lounging around in the bushes at the front.

'They're guarding it,' Shorty whispered.

'It's OK, they're asleep,' Windy replied, gesturing for Shorty to follow him round to the back of the loft. 'We'll break in here instead. Shhhhhh!' he warned, adding:

'Saw . . .'

'Saw what?' asked Shorty.

'Saw a hole in the wall,'. Windy whispered.

'Where is it? Where's the hole?' Shorty asked. 'Oh, I see — saw!' he said with a giggle, as he opened their burglar's tool bag and produced a saw.

Windy then sawed a hole in the back wall of the loft until it was large enough for him to crawl through. Then inside, fighting his way past the nest boxes, food vessels and corn bins, he grabbed the only occupant off her perch and handed her out through the hole to Shorty, outside.

'Here she is. Put her in the basket.'

'Right.'

They crept off into the darkness without disturbing Cedric and Dustin, and neither of the Muscles realized a saw had been used, as each Muscle thought it was the noise of the other Muscle snoring! The Scunner and Tub reached the loft and found Cedric and Dustin fast asleep, and Slow Flo gone.

'They've taken her,' the Scunner said. 'We've foiled them. Good! We can waken the Muscles now and go home.'

Next morning – the day of the race – the Scunner, Tub and Cedric dropped Dustin off at Chop's office, still complete with city suit, bowler hat, briefcase and umbrella to continue with his 'VAT work'. Then they drove off in the Scunner's car to the secret loft where Fast Lass had been billeted overnight. But when they arrived there it was empty.

'Oh no! She's gone! Some dirty thief's nicked her!' the Scunner groaned.

'Windy?' said Tub.

'No, the windae's intact, no one came in that way. Oh, I see what you mean – Windy? Yeah, d'you think he and Shorty nicked her? But how did they know she was here?'

Then he saw the anonymous note pinned to one of the perches.

'What's this?' he said, and read: 'I SAW YOU BRING YOUR BIRD HERE. BUT I'VE GOT HER. SHE WON'T WIN THE RACE NOW – MINE WILL!' And it was signed: 'FELLOW FANCIER'.

'What are we going to do?' Tub asked. 'Newcastle's going to kill us for letting her get stolen.'

'Aye,' the Scunner agreed, quietly. 'And I'm liable

to have to thump Clyde's big hard knuckles with my weak wee chin. Gulp! What'll we do?'

'We'll have to find another lookalike,' Cedric said.

'But there *isn't* another one!' the Scunner screeched. 'Look at all the bother we had yesterday just finding *one* lookalike, never mind another one.'

'Yeah, and the race starts in a couple of hours,' Cedric reminded him – as if he needed reminding.

'Where are we going to find a replacement now?' the Scunner asked in a panic-stricken voice. 'We've been round every loft in town to get the only one there is that looks like Fast Lass. So what do we do?'

Tub snapped his fingers. 'Chisbury! The deep-freeze pigeon!'

'Have you gone completely bonkers, Tub? That's the craziest suggestion you've ever made. Substituting a dead pigeon for a live one – and the race favourite, too! You're out of your tiny mind!'

Tub shrugged. 'But what else can we do, uncle?'

'Aye, you're right, I suppose. But how do we make it fly?'

Then it occurred to him. Inventor Black's new invention – the catapult! *That* could make it fly!

'Catapults!' he cried, excitedly, then went on to tell Tub and Cedric how they could do it.

'But will it work?' Cedric asked him.

'Aye, of course,' he replied, with confidence. 'We'll each position ourselves, with a catapult, at the places we think Chisbury's going to land each time. No problem. We've just got to pinch Black's catapults.'

'But how will we know where to position ourselves?' Tub asked. 'How will we know how far Chisbury'll fly each time?'

'That's a good question,' the Scunner said, and gave it some thought. 'After we grab the catapults we'll go up to the common and try them out and see how far they shoot Chisbury, O K?'

10 Batty Hatty!

The Scunner, Tub and Cedric drove to Black's cottage, which was unoccupied, and stole six of the catapults. Then Cedric, from force of habit, lifted the silent flute off a bench, although he didn't recognize it, having forgotten that Tub had mentioned it.

'I wonder what this is,' he muttered as they left the cottage.

He put it to his mouth and blew it.

'Wow!' he gasped as half a dozen dogs near by began waltzing around as if they'd gone potty.

Tub realized what it was.

'It's that silent flute I was telling you about,' he said, as Cedric put it in his pocket.

They drove to the common and experimented with the catapults at full strength, until they knew approximately how far each shot would project the frozen pigeon. Then, after the final shot, they retrieved Chisbury and the Scunner took charge of it.

'Right, I can now work out where it'll land each time and make my plans accordingly,' he said.

They drove back to the loft in the allotments. But on arrival they were met by Bony, who had spotted the hole in the back wall of the loft – and the fact that the bird had flown!

'Oh . . . er . . . hello, Bony,' the Scunner said. 'Um . . . ah . . . it's a good day for the race, isn't it?'

'Never mind the small talk,' he snapped. 'What's happened here? Where's Fast Lass? She's safe, I hope.'

'Aye, of course she is, she-she's f-fine,' the Scunner stuttered, nervously.

'Let me see her, then,' Bony demanded. 'Newcastle's too busy with his first concert, so he sent me along to check on her. So where is she?'

'Well . . . ah . . . um . . . er . . .' the Scunner began and then decided he'd better confess.

There was no point in trying to hide the truth from Bony, he would have to know all about it sooner or later and it might as well be sooner. So he told him everything, consoling himself with the thought that Clyde wasn't there, so his clobbering would be deferred until later.

Bony was shocked speechless by the Scunner's confession, until the Scunner added:

'We're going to replace her with Chisbury.'

'Oh well, that's all right then.' Bony cheered up again at that, until the Scunner showed him what Chisbury was!

'What? You're replacing her with a frozen pigeon from a deep freeze?' he stormed.

'We've no option, we've got nothing else. Chisbury'll have to fly in the race whether we like it or not.'

'You're joking!' Bony screeched, grabbing him by the lapels. 'Bird-brain! How d'you intend making a frozen bird fly in a race?'

82

'Och, don't worry, that problem's under control,' the Scunner assured him, and explained how he proposed using the catapults to make the pigeon fly.

'What we've got to do is shoot Chisbury off in a catapult from the start, in Chisleton, which we'll call "Point A". Then we'll shoot it off from where it lands at "Point B", to "Point C", where it lands again, and so on. And we carry on doing that, right round the circular course till it completes it and gets to the finishing line in Chisleton.'

'But why bother with all that?' Bony asked. 'You could hang about till the rest of the pigeons are on their way back and *then* catapult Chisbury from near the finishing line. That would save you wandering about all over the countryside with catapults.'

'That wouldn't work,' the Scunner explained. 'There's check points all round the course, with officials making sure no one cheats. So the only way is for Chisbury to fly past them with the other pigeons.'

'O K, but remember,' Bony warned him, 'Chisbury must *win* the race, frozen or not! Newcastle's prize money! And his big bet!'

The Scunner smiled confidently. 'Don't worry, it'll win all right. It'll have to start a few minutes after the others, but it'll soon catch up. Then it'll overtake them, on its rocket-powered flight.'

'Well if it doesn't win it'll be the worse for you. Clyde will blacken your eye, then I'll blacken your name – in criminal circles. Or should that be *whiten* your name, seeing you're a black-hearted villain already?' he said. Then, after a few seconds' thought, he added: 'How are you going to explain, at the finishing line, that the winner's dead?'

'Och, I'll just say it died of excitement at winning!' the Scunner said, cheerfully.

As Bony walked off down the path he shouted back: 'You've pulled some stunts in your time, but racing a frozen pigeon's the limit. That takes the biscuit.'

The Scunner, Tub and Cedric left the allotments, taking Chisbury with them. A frozen pigeon, after all, doesn't need a loft to live in – it would be just as happy in the Scunner's pocket!

'Is it time for me to go and kidnap the Duchess of Oz?' Cedric asked.

'Aye, off you go or the Bashers'll beat you to it,' the Scunner said, handing him his car keys.

As the Bashers were due to board the train and waylay the Duchess at Paddleton, the station before Chisleton, Cedric would waylay her at Poshtown, the stop before that, so that he could pull the stunt before they did. Then, after bringing her to Chisleton in the Scunner's car, they would hand her over to Scoundrel, to prove that the Scunner's group, with his initiative, had outdone the Bashers' group.

Cedric set off and, to begin with, everything went according to plan. He drove to Poshtown, boarded the train and contacted the Duchess, who was wearing a large, black cloak.

'What?' she said. 'The line's blocked and I've to go by car?'

'Yeah.'

'And you've come for *me* specially?' She seemed surprised.

'Yeah, that's right.'

She didn't need any coaxing. 'OK, let's go.'

She jumped out of her seat, pushed him aside and leapt out of the compartment and off the train.

Cedric was taken aback.

'Cor! I didn't know Duchesses behaved like that,' he muttered. 'Mind you, she's the first Duchess I've ever met.'

But this *wasn't* the first Duchess he had met, for this wasn't the Duchess of Oz – this was someone else!

The trouble was, he had spoken to the first woman he had come across in a First Class compartment who looked as if she might be a Duchess, and hadn't stopped to ask her name. And this particular woman's name was Harriet Patti, otherwise known, to the criminal fraternity, as Batty Hatty Patti, the well-known kleptomaniac.

Hatty couldn't help herself. Or rather, she couldn't help helping herself! For, as she rushed along the station platform with Cedric, towards the car parked outside, she grabbed everything she could lay her hands on – parcels of mail, magazines from the bookstall, pot plants from the station display – and whipped them all under her large, black, voluminous cloak.

'Huh? What're you doing?' he asked.

And he repeated this question as they drove towards Chisleton and he saw a road atlas and six audio tapes disappearing from a shelf into the large shoplifter's pockets inside her cloak.

They met the Scunner and Tub in Chisleton, as arranged, but before they could take the 'Duchess' to Scoundrel she spotted Chisbury's Department Store.

'I wanna go in there!' she cried, her eyes lighting up.

'Ah . . . um . . . later, madam,' the Scunner said.

'Now!'

And she proceeded to shoplift everything in sight!

'Do all Duchesses do that, Uncle?' Tub asked.

'Search me!' he replied – which was the wrong thing to say with Hatty around! 'Hey! Take your hands out of my pockets, madam!'

He glanced round the store to see if anyone else had noticed Hatty's habits, but no one had.

'Maybe her husband, the Duke, is penniless and sends her out shoplifting!' he murmured.

And if no one in the store noticed Hatty it was just sheer luck, for her cloak was already bulging to capacity and the Scunner was becoming concerned about it.

11   The Duchess of Oz!

The Basher Brothers encountered the real Duchess of Oz on the train, told her the line was blocked, persuaded her to leave it and proceeded to kidnap her, as arranged.

'No problem,' Basher said.

But their problems began when they got her back to the college. They found a note pinned to the front door of the house telling them that Scoundrel was in Chisleton with the other pupils, and the door was locked.

'Oh, isn't this fair dinkum, Bruce?' the Duchess said, admiring the house.

'We'd best put her into that walled garden at the back till we can get her into the house,' Basher suggested.

'Yeah,' Crasher agreed, 'it's got a gate wot locks.'

'Ah, this is truly dinkum,' she went on, looking at the show of daffodils in the garden. 'You see, darlings, it's such a joy for me to be here in the Old Country. England. Britain. Home of the dear, dear Queen of Aussieland. Oz. 'Stralia. Oh, but I was forgetting – she's your queen too, isn't she?' She giggled gaily.

'She'll be safe enough in here,' Basher said, looking at the wall which surrounded the large garden. That's what he thought!

'And just look at all those daffies. They're glorious . . .'

'No, they're not Gloria's,' Crasher said.

'No, Bruce, glorious,' she laughed. 'They're darling.
Stupendous. I must just gather some. May I? A few?'

She ran into the garden and gathered up armfuls of
the flowers.

The Bashers locked her in and went to sit on the
front steps of the house, to await Scoundrel's return.
But after a while Basher thought he'd better check how
the Duchess was getting on in the garden.

'She gone! She's disappeared!' he yelled, running
back to tell his brother.

She had found a break in the high wall, had squeezed
through it and had trotted down the driveway to the
gate. And when the Bashers got there they found her in
the act of handing a daffodil to every passerby.

'G'day, sport,' she greeted each one. 'Have a daffy.
Here y'are, Bruce, take one home to your sheila.
They're beautiful, aren't they, cobber?'

'Wot you doing?' Basher asked.

'Well, Bruce,' – she called everyone Bruce! – 'I saw
the queen handing out daffies to everyone on her
birthday, on telly – she was lovely, wasn't she? So I
wanted to do the same. 'Cos I'm one of Her Majesty's
most loyal Aussie subjects. Truly.'

They persuaded her to return up the driveway to the
house again and re-enter the garden.

'When do I start the horse race, Bruce?' she asked,
smiling.

'Er . . . ah . . . um . . . we've to see our boss first,' Basher told her.

They put her back into the garden, locked the gate and sat on a seat near by, to study the sports page of the *Pij Post*.

'Who d'you think'll win the Pigeon Race, now that Windy and Shorty have nicked the favourite?' Crasher asked.

But Basher wasn't listening. He was peering through the bars of the gate into the garden.

'She's disappeared again!' he yelled.

They found her back at the gate, handing out flowers to all and sundry once more.

'G'day, Poms,' she smiled at them, 'have a daffy . . .'

'Cor,' a passing workman said, 'it's more like *her* wot's daffy, if you ask me!'

The frustrated Bashers grabbed her by the arms, but her arms were still full of daffodils which she tossed to the people outside the gate.

'What are you doing, Bruce? Here, you can't do this to a Duchess, y'know.'

'A Duchess?' a passing postman said. 'Some Duchess!'

'I *am* a Duchess,' she insisted. 'I'm the Duchess of Oz.'

'And I'm the *Wizard* of Oz!' the postman retorted.

The Bashers tried to haul her backwards up the drive, but she dropped the last few daffodils from her arms, which enabled her to get her fingers into her mouth and whistle a loud, shrill blast on them, then:

'Taxi!' she yelled, as one passed by in the street outside. 'Take me to your Pommy racecourse.'

She turned to ask the Bashers: 'Is it a horse race I'm starting, or a greyhound race?'

'It's not the races she needs to be taken to,' a woman shopper said, touching one finger to her temple, 'it's the fun house.'

'Maybe that *is* the fun house,' one of the men replied, seeing the Bashers trying to drag her – backwards! – up the drive.

They eventually managed to haul her back to the house and put her inside the walled garden again.

'Imagine her whistling with her fingers like that,' Basher said, horrified. 'It's dead common, i'nt it?'

'Yeah,' Crasher agreed, 'she's just like one of us, i'nt she?'

'I must gather more daffies. They're so dinkum, Bruce. They're truly, truly dinkum.'

Basher turned to his brother and pointed through the garden gate to the break in the wall at the far side.

'We'll have to stand here and keep our eyes on that broken bit of wall over there.'

'OK, Bruce,' Crasher said. 'Cor! She's got me at it now!'

But although they took turns at the gate, keeping their eyes on the broken wall at the side, she still managed to escape from the garden! This time she found a small door in the back wall which opened out on to the main road.

'Oh no! Where's she got to now?' Basher moaned.

'She's better at escaping than Houdini was!' Crasher groaned.

Outside, in the road, she approached passers-by again with her daffodils, and asked them to direct her to the High Street.

'I've to start a horse race, or something,' she explained, 'and I've to meet the mayor.'

'If it's a horse race you're going to,' a man laughed, 'then it's the M.A.R.E. mare you're looking for!'

'Maybe it's the Pigeon Race?' his wife suggested.

'Yes, that sounds like it, darlings,' she said, beaming.

But another passerby was suspicious of her. After all, here was a strange woman handing out flowers to everyone. But were they hers? Where had she got them? Were they stolen? What was she up to? And was she really going racing with the mayor – or the mare?

He hurried to a nearby phone box and dialled 999 and, minutes later, P C Leekie arrived in his panda car and arrested the Duchess, on suspicion of stealing the flowers.

'You've got it wrong, Bruce,' she told him, 'I'm the Duchess of Oz . . .'

'Yes, and I'm the Wiz . . .' he began.

'We've already heard that one, Bruce,' she said as he put her into the car.

The Bashers ran down the drive again, pursuing her, and they reached the gate in time to see Leekie arriving. But as they didn't want to get involved with the police they each hid behind a gate pillar until the panda car drove off.

'Well that's the end of the kidnapping,' Basher said, and Crasher shrugged.

And so the Duchess of Oz managed to escape from her kidnappers – unaware that she had been kidnapped in the first place! But instead of being a captive in the Crooks' College she now found herself a prisoner of the Pommy police!

'What's the big idea, Bruce?' she demanded.

'There's a woman going round town today nicking everything in sight. Her name's Batty Hatty Patti – and that's you.'

'What? It most certainly is not, Bruce. I'm the Duchess of Oz from beautiful Aussieland. Cuddly koalas, how often do I have to tell you? I even know the queen – well, at least I've seen her on TV!'

'Yeah, all right, Hatty.'

'Stop calling me Hatty, Bruce.'

'And you stop calling me Bruce, Hatty!' retorted Leekie as he pushed her into cell No. 1.

And Muggins, on hearing of the arrest, agreed with Leekie.

'Yes, it's definitely Batty Hatty,' he declared. 'Nicking daffodils, was she?'

'Look, cobber – copper – I'm not this Hatty woman. I'm the Duchess of Oz. So kindly let me out of your Pommy prison.'

'Listen, Hatty . . .'

Muggins made the mistake of approaching her cell to speak to her and she whacked him in the face with her last bunch of daffodils as he came close to the bars.

Then she remembered something she had in her hand-bag that should clinch the matter.

'Look, Bruce,' she said, pulling out a handful of Duchess-like jewellery to show him. 'I wouldn't have these if I wasn't a Duchess, would I?'

'Huh, they're phonies,' he snorted.

'They are *not* phonies,' she yelled. 'My hubby the Duke had to shear a lot of sheep to be able to buy these! And it was *sheer* hard work, I can tell you.'

'Well if they're not phonies they're the proceeds of your shop-lifting activities, Hatty.'

'How dare you, you nasty Pom. Let me out of here, d'you hear?' She banged on the bars of her cell. 'If you don't let me out at once I'll report you to my very good friend – Her Majesty.'

'Huh, Mrs Thatcher won't help you,' Muggins said, as he waved the cell keys at her defiantly.

'Huh? Who's Mrs Thatchah?' she asked as she continued to bang on the bars.

12   Dumpling in Charge

PC Dumpling entered Muggins's office and the Inspector looked up.

'Ah, Dumpling, can you cope with the station on your own this afternoon? Leekie and I and some of the other coppers want to go to the replay of the cricket match.'

'Oh, yes, sir, certainly, sir,' Dumpling replied, eager to prove he was up to being a policeman in the Chisleton Police Force.

Muggins left his office and popped his head into the other rooms. 'Right lads! Dumpling's in charge. Let's go.'

They all trooped out of the station and jumped into their panda cars, leaving Dumpling in control of the station and of the Duchess of Oz, who was still bitterly complaining in her cell.

'I'm *not* Fatty Hatty, I tell you, Bruce,' she yelled, but everyone just ignored her.

'Now remember, Dumpling,' Muggins said, on his way out, 'this is your big chance to redeem yourself for all your earlier mistakes. But if you don't make a success of it you'll have to hand in your handcuffs and leave the force. O K?'

'O K, sir,' Dumpling replied, praying silently that

nothing terrible would happen while he was left on his own.

'D'you think it's all right leaving Dumbo in charge of the nick?' Leekie asked, as he drove them to the cricket ground.

'Relax,' Muggins replied. 'What could happen?'

'Well, there's the Pigeon Race, for a start,' Leekie said. 'It's on today, remember. He could have trouble there.'

'Nonsense,' said Muggins, confidently. 'It's held every year and we've never had trouble yet.'

'But I've heard there are a few mobs in town, hanging around somewhere,' Leekie replied.

He was referring to Scoundrel's College and its pupils, although he was rather vague, as he knew very little about them. And he didn't realize he had been at the gates of the college when he arrested the Duchess, and could almost have touched some of the members of the mobs he was talking about.

'And *they* might cause trouble at the race,' Leekie persisted, as they arrived at the cricket ground.

'Don't worry, Leekie,' said an untroubled Muggins, as he settled down to watch the match. 'Here, have a toffee.' He offered Leekie the bag. 'And stop worrying. What could possibly happen? All right, so there was a female felon on the loose, but we caught her, didn't we?'

That's what *he* thought!

Willard and his team-mates were not looking forward

to the replay of the match against the Snobbers for, even with their extra coaching, there was no way they were going to have a chance against the bigger, stronger boys.

'Oh-oh, here they come,' he moaned, just before two o'clock, when the Snobbers' team arrived in their minibus again.

They looked snooty, smirked a lot and didn't hide the fact that they intended carving up the Chisleton Boys' Club cricket team once and for all.

'I don't know why we had to come all this way again,' Timothy Toff complained. 'We should have been awarded the match without having to play you little tykes again.'

'Yes,' Desmond added, 'and you know you haven't a chance against us.'

'Huh, cheek!' Willard muttered, although he had to admit that Desmond was quite right.

He entered the pavilion's dressing-room and looked round to count his players.

'Oh no, Bobby's missing.'

'He's chickened out,' Willard's pal yelled.

'I don't blame him,' Willard muttered under his breath. 'I wish *I'd* been able to chicken out. But I'm the captain and I've got to be here! Huh!' He looked around for their twelfth man. 'Where's Phil?'

'He's chickened out, too!' his pal yelled again.

'Huh!' Willard murmured. 'We'd be better playing this match in a poultry farm!'

'I only wish your gran could play for us,' his pal

said, wistfully. 'It's a pity she's not a boy, isn't it?'

'That's it!' Willard snapped his fingers. 'She *is* a boy!'

'Pardon?'

'An honorary boy! We made her an honorary member of the club, remember? She passed the initiation test. So she *can* play for us!'

'Yippee!' the team cheered.

Willard rushed from the dressing-room to tell Super Gran, who had just arrived with Edison.

'Play for the Boys' Club, Willie?' she cried. 'Jings, I can't wait. Do I bowl first or bat first?'

'And just wait till I tell the Snobbers you're playing,' he said. 'I can't wait to see their faces!'

But he was surprised at the Snobbers' response to the news.

'What? Your grandmama, playing cricket – *trying* to play cricket! – against us, the Snobbers, the best Boys' Club team in England? You're joking!'

Then Timothy practically threw him out of their dressing-room, while a delighted Super Gran went about asking:

'Have you got such a thing as tartan leg-guards?'

Willard couldn't understand the Snobbers never having heard of Super Gran. After all, they came from Poshtown, which was only about twelve miles away, and he thought, as she did, that everyone had heard of her by now.

He supposed they hadn't heard of her because they

lived in their own little world, surrounded by servants and mixing only with people of their own class. Although surely even those sort of people, he thought, had heard of her?

'Well, they soon will hear of her,' he muttered to himself.

But Super Gran was having problems!

'Crivvens, I can't find any tartan pads,' she said. 'I'll just have to make do with ordinary white ones.'

'It won't matter what colour they are, Gran,' Willard said, with a grin. 'As long as you get us plenty of runs when you put them on, that's all!'

All that morning Dustin had pretended to do his V A T work in Mr Chop's office. But as he didn't know what he was supposed to do he spent all his time doodling on a blank blotting-paper pad. And he discovered that it's harder work trying to *look* busy than it is actually doing the work!

As he doodled he wondered how long he would have to wait and 'work' before he'd be able to snatch Chop's safe keys.

But at lunchtime Chop rose from his desk and crossed the office to take his jacket off the coatstand.

'Ah, Mr . . . er . . . Dustbin,' he began, wondering again about someone having a name like 'Dustbin', 'it's my lunchtime now, and then . . . um . . . er . . . I'll be taking the afternoon off for a cricket match.'

'Huh? A cricket match?' gasped Dustin, realizing that this could be his big chance to get at the safe.

'It's the Boys' Club who are playing and I'm a former member, so I want to support them.' He suddenly looked concerned, and frowned. 'Do *you* want to see the match?'

'No,' Dustin said, 'I hate cricket.'

'What . . .!'

Dustin thought Chop was going to have a heart attack at the idea of someone – an Englishman! – not being interested in cricket.

'I'll just stay here and get on wiv my V A T stuff,' he said.

What he really meant was: 'I'll stay here and rob your safe!'

'Oh well, I'll see you later, when I return.'

'That's what *you* think!' Dustin murmured, under his breath, as he helped him on with his jacket.

But Dustin wasn't merely being helpful – he was actually taking the chance to slip the office keys out of the man's pocket!

'See you later, Mr . . . er . . . Dustbin.'

'Yeah, *much* later,' Dustin laughed, looking at the keys and grinning happily at the one marked 'Safe'.

The Scunner would have been proud of him if he'd seen that nifty pocket-picking, he thought.

He followed Chop out of the office and saw him driving off in his car. Then he heard the factory siren wailing, telling the workers it was lunchtime. But he still had to wait another half an hour before Chop's secretary left for lunch.

'Naw,' he told her when she looked in on him, 'I'm not going just now. I'm . . . er . . . ah . . . working on.'

Then, as soon as she left, he pulled the parcel out from under his desk, ripped the paper off it and took out his 'Arctic' outfit. He put it on over his city suit and pulled its hood over his bowler hat, which he had put on! Then, taking his rolled umbrella and his briefcase – to put the stolen money in – he walked through the deserted factory to the cold store.

As he put his hand on the handle of the large heavy steel door he saw it had an automatic security-locking device. And even Dustin, dumb as he was, realized he'd better leave the door open behind him, in case he accidentally locked himself in.

'Here goes,' he grinned, pleased with himself, as he pulled his snow goggles over his eyes.

Inside the store he hurried towards the safe in the far corner and unlocked the door with Chop's key. Everything was going according to plan.

'The Scunner'll be pleased with me,' he said, as the door swung open and he smiled happily in anticipation.

13   It's SAFE in the Arctic!

Mr Chop, eating his lunch in a restaurant, put his hand in his pocket to make sure he had his wallet with him.

'Help! The office keys! They're gone!'

He searched all his pockets and remembered he'd had them just before he left his office.

'I must've lost them on the way here,' he said and began to panic. 'If someone's found them they could rob the safe.'

He rushed to the restaurant's call box to phone the Police Station and report his loss.

'What's that? Lost your safe keys?' said P C Dumpling, answering the call and taking down the details. 'Leave it to me. I'll investigate it right away.'

Panicking as much as Chop, he jumped up and down excitedly and dropped the phone on the floor. This was his first case since taking charge of the station and he wanted to do his very best.

'If I go to his factory and find the keys it'll make up for all those mistakes I've made.'

He rushed from the station, putting on his special helmet as he ran. Then he pressed its button and the blue light on the top began revolving and the police siren wailed 'Ee-aw, ee-aw, ee-aw . . .'

'Here I come,' he yelled, startling passersby.

But he startled them even more when he twirled his truncheon as he ran along the back streets towards Chop's factory, because it kept slipping from his hand and flying through the air, narrowly missing innocent bystanders!

'Hey, look out!' they cried, trying to dodge it.

He arrived at the main office door to find it had been locked by the secretary with *her* keys, on her way out to lunch. So Chop's lost keys weren't an immediate problem.

'I'd better check the factory entrance though, just in case,' he said.

He found it unlocked and, entering the premises to investigate, he spotted the open door of the cold store.

''Ello, 'ello, 'ello, I'd better check this, too,' he said.

Inside, Dustin was lifting bundles of banknotes out of the safe and was drooling over them.

'Lovely loot,' he murmured. 'The Scunner'll be pleased.'

A sudden noise at the door made him jump.

'Wot's that? Who's there?'

As Dumpling entered the room there was a slight click from behind him. He spotted, through the cold mist, the figure in the Arctic gear standing at the safe in the far corner, with the money in his hand.

'Gotcha!' he cried, in triumph.

Dustin was startled by Dumpling's sudden appearance from behind one of the hanging carcasses, his notebook and pen in one hand and his truncheon in the other.

'Huh?' he said.

Dumpling cleared his throat nervously and declared:

'You're . . . er, ah . . . under . . . um . . . arrest and . . . ah, er . . . anything you . . . um, anything you . . . er . . .'

'Anything you say . . .' Dustin prompted.

'Oh yes, anything you say . . . um . . . er . . .'

'Will be taken down . . .'

'I remember – will be taken down and used . . . um . . . er?' He appealed to Dustin to continue his prompting.

'In evidence,' Dustin sighed.

'Yes, in evidence . . .'

Dustin had to help the constable make his arresting speech, but then Dustin had heard it often enough before!

'Wot they teaching you young coppers in Fuzz College nowadays?' he asked.

Dumpling had been struggling to write things down in his notebook but his fingers were rapidly freezing.

'I need your name and . . .' He stopped to blow on his hands.

It was all right for the villain, he thought, he was warmly wrapped up and was wearing mittens.

But Dustin had helped the rookie policeman all he was going to help him. He now intended doing a bunk.

He suddenly dashed past him and reached the door – only to realize what the loud, ominous click had been just before Dumpling had appeared. It was the heavy steel security-door shutting behind him as he entered.

'Yeeks! We're trapped!' he yelled.

'What d'you mean, trapped?' Dumpling asked.

'You must've shut the door behind you when you came in.'

'Oh no!' Dumpling groaned.

Dustin's normally inane grin froze on his face, not only with the cold, but also with the gravity of the situation!

Soon they were both frozen stiff as more and more snow and icicles appeared on their hair and eyebrows; soon their ears and noses would be covered with it, too. And Dumpling was especially vulnerable as he wasn't wearing protective clothing.

'You l . . . look like "Sc . . . cott of the Ant . . . tarc-tic",' Dumpling said, through chattering teeth, to Dustin, sitting near the safe, toying with the stolen money.

'Yeah, well after locking us in here you're the "clot of the Antarctic"!' Dustin retorted as the banknotes fluttered from his frozen fingers.

'How are w . . . we g . . . going to g . . . get out of h . . . here?' Dumpling asked.

He was sitting propped up against the wall, hugging himself to keep warm.

'How should I know? You're the fuzz. What did they teach you at Fuzz College about escaping from cold stores?'

'N . . . not a l . . . lot,' Dumpling admitted. 'I d . . . don't th . . . think they c . . . covered c . . . cold sores, I mean, c . . . cold stores.'

'We could do with Super Gran to break down the door for us,' Dustin said.

'B . . . but sh . . . she's at the c . . . c . . . cricket m . . . match,' Dumpling said. 'And s . . . so's M . . . Muggins and L . . . Leekie and the others.'

Dustin's face lit up and resumed something of its usual idiotic grin as an idea came to him.

'Has Leekie got his walkie-talkie thing with him?'

'His p . . . p . . . personal r . . . radio? Y . . . yes, he w . . . will have,' Dumpling said.

'Put a call through to him,' Dustin said, 'on *your* walkie-talkie. And get him to send Super Gran here.'

Dumpling's face brightened through the snow which now covered it, as his frozen fingers grabbed at his personal radio and, with difficulty, switched it on.

Then, summoning up sufficient strength to fight the cold, he yelled: 'H . . . help . . . L . . . Leekie . . . S . . . Super G . . . Gran . . . D . . . Dumpling . . . L . . . locked in . . . Ch . . . Ch . . . Chop's F . . . Factory . . . C . . . c . . . cold s . . . s . . . store . . . H . . . help . . .'

The cricket match began, but for the Chisleton team there was no success. They batted first but despite their coaching session they didn't fare any better than they had done in the first match. Willard and his opening partner were both out for a duck – again! And the rest of their side followed suit and, in no time at all, their score was nothing for nine wickets!

Then Super Gran emerged from the pavilion.

'Jings, I'm raring to go!' she said.

'Let's hope *she* puts on some runs,' Willard's pal said. 'If she doesn't we've had it. She's the last man – sorry, woman – in.'

She skipped down the pavilion steps to the welcoming applause of Muggins, Leekie and the other policemen and spectators.

'You'll have to keep facing the bowling, Gran,' Willard told her. 'Little Sammy's your partner and he'll be out for a duck if *he's* got to face it. You're our only chance.'

'Rightio, Willie.'

She marched to the wicket to join her partner and she worked out what she'd have to do to keep facing the bowling, while the Snobbers, watching her approach the crease, guffawed loudly.

'Who does she think *she* is?' Timothy laughed.

'These peasants are playing that old biddy against *us*?' Desmond asked. He could hardly believe it.

D. Red-Locks rubbed the ball on his trouser leg as Super Gran took guard. 'I shouldn't bother too much, dear, I'll have you out before you can blink.'

But instead of his usual fast delivery he bowled a soft, slow ball to give her a chance. And he was utterly amazed when she hit it to the boundary for a four. But he was even more utterly amazed when she put a really big effort into the next ball and thumped it clear over the boundary for a six.

'Huh?' he gasped, and decided to speed up his bowling to its normal tempo again. She had made a fool of him by mistreating his bowling in that way.

But it didn't matter how fast the demon bowler bowled: she was able to thump it all over the pitch. And by the end of that over she had scored twenty-seven runs, in fours and sixes, although she deliberately scored only a single on the last ball, to ensure that she was at the correct end to receive the other bowler for the next over. And this turned out to be Timothy Toff himself.

Seeing the direction in which she had hit D. Red-Locks' bowling to the boundary, Timothy moved his fielders around, to prevent her doing it again. But she merely aimed her Super-thumps in a different direc-tion – and went on clouting the ball towards the boundary for fours and sixes, this time scoring twenty-nine runs.

And again she ensured, at the end of the over, that she would still face the bowling, to keep little Sammy away from it.

And once again she thumped the West Indian boy's bowling all over the pitch, carefully choosing places where there were no fielders, and making all eleven Snobbers more and more angry. In this over she scored five sixes and a single, making thirty-one and giving Chisleton a score of eighty-seven in total.

And, much to the Snobbers' embarrassment and humiliation, she went on scoring for another three overs, until Chisleton's score stood at one hundred and forty-four. Then she hit one last six, to make it one hundred and fifty.

'That's a nice round figure,' she said as she gave Willard the nod to declare their innings closed.

He did so, reluctantly, as she walked off the pitch to thunderous applause, while her partner, little Sammy, was equally proud of the part he'd played in the last-wicket stand by running between the wickets while Super Gran was scoring her single runs!

'But Gran, the Snobbers could easily reach that,' Willard pointed out.

'Don't worry,' she assured him, 'I'll have the wee bachles out long before they make one hundred and fifty – once I start to do my Super-dynamic bowling. Easy-peasy!'

'I hope so,' Willard replied, not entirely convinced.

'Of course I will, Willie,' she insisted. 'What could go wrong?'

'I dunno. I've just got a feeling, that's all.'

The Snobbers went in to bat and Super Gran started out on her bowling career by getting their first two batsmen out for a duck, in successive balls. But it was just then, as she was getting into her stride, that she got her call for help from Dumpling in the cold store.

14 Two Rescues

Muggins and Leekie, sitting together in the stand, applauded Super Gran's second duck.

'One more wicket and she's got a hat-trick,' Muggins said.

But Leekie's mind wasn't entirely on the match!

'I wonder how Dumpling's getting on by himself in the nick?'

'Oh, he'll be all right,' Muggins assured him. 'Just as long as he doesn't let that old pest Batty Hatty out of her cell, that's all.' He was referring, of course, to the Duchess of Oz.

Suddenly they heard Dumpling's voice coming through, feebly, on Leekie's personal radio.

'Help . . . Leekie . . . Super Gran . . . Dumpling . . . Locked in . . . Chop's Factory cold store . . . Help . . .'

Super Gran, standing near the boundary while awaiting the arrival of Timothy, the Snobbers' third man in, heard the SOS.

'Jings, that's terrible!' She threw the ball to Willard – who ducked in case it brained him! 'I'll have to rescue him!'

'Oh! Gra-an, must you?' he yelled. 'Why can't Muggins and Leekie and that lot go and help him?'

''Cos I'm faster, that's why!' she retorted as she ran from the pitch.

She zoomed from the cricket ground into the road outside, along the High Street, then down towards Chop's factory. She entered, located the cold store and yanked its solid-steel door open. Then, finding the room full of icy mist, she Super-blew a passage through it to let her see Dustin sitting in front of the safe, some of the banknotes still clutched in his frozen fingers.

'Good old Super Gran,' he said, grinning inanely at her and offering her a handful of banknotes as a reward.

'Tut-tut, Dustin,' she said.

He thought she was saying this wasn't enough so he offered her two handfuls of notes instead!

'Tut-tut, shame on you.'

'Oh, all right then, take the lot!' he yelled, throwing all the money at her.

'What I mean is – it's not yours to hand out.'

'Aw, but –'

'Where's Dumpling?' She looked round the store and spotted him huddled against the wall. 'Oh, there he is!'

He nodded slightly and stiffly held out a pair of ice-covered handcuffs which she attached to Dustin's wrists.

As the safe key was covered in ice and the door couldn't be locked, she stuffed all the banknotes into Dustin's briefcase. Then, after slinging his umbrella over her arm and slinging *him* over one shoulder and

115

Dumpling over the other, she lugged them from the cold store, closed the door behind her and carried them *and* the briefcase to the Police Station.

'Mr Chop can collect his money there, eh, PC Dumpling?' she said. 'It'll be safer than leaving it lying about the cold store.'

But as she hurried from the factory she didn't notice the two men who watched her from behind a bench. They were Bill and Wally from the Crooks' College, on their safe-breaking project.

They had found out the safe was in the cold store and had arrived there to rob it just as Super Gran emerged carrying the policeman and the 'Arctic explorer'.

'Whew! Did you see that?' Bill gasped.

'Yeah, I saw it – but I don't believe it!' Wally said, then:

'Look!' Bill yelled when they opened the door, entered the store and found the empty safe. 'She's taken the money with her!'

At the Police Station she deposited Dumpling and Dustin in the middle of the floor.

'Th . . . thanks, Super Gran,' said Dumpling, having by now thawed out sufficiently to speak to her.

He got to his feet, put the briefcase into a safe and locked Dustin in cell No. 2, next to the Duchess of Oz, who was still protesting loudly.

'Let me out of here, Bruce!' she yelled. 'And tell that Inspector Muggins of yours that I . . .'

'Jings! Muggins!' Super Gran exclaimed. That reminded her that he was at the cricket match – where

she should be, helping the boys' team. 'I'll have to run, I forgot about them. Can you manage, PC Dumpling?'

'Yes, thanks, Super Gran.'

'I wonder what the score is?' she said.

'We can easily find out. I'll call Leekie up on his personal radio and ask him.'

'Good idea,' she said, then: 'Hello, Rupert,' when he came through on the radio. 'What's the score?'

'It's bad news, Super Gran. No more wickets have fallen since you left – but Toff and his partner have scored thirty.'

'Right, I'm on my way,' she yelled as she threw the radio back to Dumpling and sped out of the door.

But by the time she reached the cricket ground the Snobbers' score had reached forty.

'Och, don't worry, Willie,' she assured him as she ran across the pitch, rolled up her cardigan sleeves, took the ball and prepared to bowl again. 'I'll have the rest of these cheeky wee scunners out in no time at all.'

Then, after rubbing the ball on her cardigan, in imitation of what she'd seen D. Red-Locks doing, she ran up and bowled – and sent Timothy's bails metres into the air.

'Howsat, ref?' she yelled.

'Out!' said the umpire.

'But, umpire,' Toff appealed, 'that claim should be disallowed. She called you "ref" instead of "umpire"!'

But Mr Bowler ignored his pleas and the disgruntled Timothy slouched back to the pavilion in a huff.

118

Then she bowled again and got Desmond out. And then she bowled a third Snobber out.

'That's her hat-trick this time,' Muggins yelled as he, Leekie and the other spectators cheered and applauded her performance.

'What did I tell you, Willie?' she said as they waited for the next batsman to reach the wicket. 'It's easy-peasy.'

But it was just then that she got her second call for help – from the Duchess of Oz.

The Duchess, having seen Super Gran in action at the Police Station, decided that her only means of escape, or rescue, was through her. So, to achieve this, she tricked Dumpling into entering her cell.

'Ooh, Bruce, I'm ill,' she lied.

She threw herself on the floor and when he opened the door and rushed in she caught him unawares, grabbed his personal radio, switched it on and yelled:

'Help! SOS – Save Oz, Super Gran! Duchess locked in Chisleton nick! Quick! Save me! My life's in danger! Truly!'

She had previously seen how he had used the radio and was sure she'd got the message through before he grabbed it back from her. He scrambled out of the cell, locked it behind him and thought that that was the last he would hear of the matter.

But Super Gran, at the match, heard the SOS coming through Leekie's radio loud and clear – at the top of the Duchess's voice!

'Jings! Another cry for help? I'll have to go, Willie!'

119

'Oh no, Gran,' Willard moaned. 'You can't go, we need you.'

'But that Duchess needs me too, Willie. Her life's in danger! I've got to go.'

'But, Gran . . .' he pleaded.

But she was half-way out of the ground by now and heard neither Willard nor Muggins, who yelled:

'Stop, Super Gran! She's not a Duchess – she's a shop-lifter!'

And the other spectators were astonished to see her racing from the pitch once again.

'*Now* where's she off to?' they asked each other, and shrugged.

She borrowed a pair of roller skates from a small boy outside the ground and whizzed along the road, reached the Police Station, whipped them off, dashed inside and confronted Dumpling.

'I got an S O S from a Duchess . . .' she began, but he interrupted and pointed across to her cell.

'No, it was Batty Hatty over there. She claims to be the Duchess of Oz but she's really a shop-lifter.'

'I am not! I keep telling you, Bruce.'

She stood at her cell door, shaking the bars.

'Super Gran, I appeal to you. Only you – you dear, dinkum, "wee" Scottish person – can help me.'

'But what can *I* do?'

'You can *prove* I'm the Duchess of Oz. And you can tell this Pommy policeman I'm not this horrid Batty person, and get me out of here. You must. I'm due to meet your mayor.'

'Huh! Mayor!' snorted the disbelieving Dumpling.

'I am, Bruce,' she insisted. 'I've got some sort of a race to start. A greyhound race, or something. At three o'clock. And I've got to be there bang on time.'

'Greyhound race?' Super Gran said, puzzled, then a thought struck her. 'Could it be the Pigeon Race?'

'Yes, that's it, I remember now,' she said.

Super Gran went over to the cell and read the Duchess's mind. Then she turned to Dumpling.

'Yes, she *is* the Duchess of Oz, all right. You'd better release her.'

But Dumpling shook his head. 'It's more than my job's worth. If I release *her* Muggins'll release *me* – from the force!'

'No problem!' cried Super Gran. 'We'll call him up at the match and ask his permission, OK?' But that reminded her again. 'Oh jings, the match! I wonder what the score is now?'

Dumpling called up Leekie at the cricket ground once more, to speak to Muggins.

'Ask him if he'll release me too!' Dustin's voice rang out, from cell No. 2.

'You're not on,' Dumpling snapped.

'Oh well, it was worth a try, wasn't it?' He grinned.

But it took some persuasion on Super Gran's part before Muggins agreed to release the Duchess.

'She's to start the Pigeon Race, and she's due there now,' Super Gran explained.

'Oh, well, all right,' he eventually agreed. 'And now

may I get back to watching this match – this debacle of a match!'

'Oh aye, that reminds me, what's the score?'

'Seventy!' he moaned. 'And still no more wickets down. When on earth are you coming back here to start bowling out some more of these little perishing snobs? Huh?'

'I'm leaving right now, Inspector. Just as soon as Dumpling lets the Duchess out of her cell and I take her along the High Street, to the mayor.'

15 Pigeon Race Rogues

As Dumpling released the Duchess, the Police Station door swung open and P C Peasea attempted to bring in a woman he had arrested. But he couldn't get her through the single door and had to open the double doors, to enable her to get her huge, bulging, loot-filled cloak through.

'Who's this?' Dumpling asked.

'Batty Hatty Patti,' P C Peasea said.

'I'm not,' she denied. 'I'm the Duchess of Ozland or Austria – or somewhere!'

It was so obvious that she didn't know who she was supposed to be that no one listened to her and Super Gran didn't even have to read her mind to find out who she was.

Dumpling called up Muggins again on his radio.

'Good news, Spec! The real Batty Hatty's been nicked.'

'Great! But don't call me Spec!' Muggins yelled.

Super Gran grabbed the radio. 'What's the score now?'

'It's ninety,' Muggins screamed. 'Get back here at once!'

'Yes, sir.' She saluted the radio, and smiled.

'And tell Dumpling to lock up Batty Hatty in cell No. 1, in place of the Duchess.'

But when she went to pass on this instruction she found that the cell key had been mislaid and Dumpling, the Duchess and PC Peasea were searching for it. Dumpling looked for it among the phones on the desk; Peasea looked under the counter; the Duchess looked into the cell; and Batty Hatty looked – rather smug!

'Come on,' said Super Gran, holding her hand out towards her. 'Hand it over.'

'Huh?' said Hatty, looking all innocent. 'What d'you mean?'

Super Gran pointed to her hugely bulging cloak. 'It's in there somewhere, isn't it? *You*'ve got it, haven't you?'

She prodded the front of it – and about three hundred assorted objects cascaded out on to the floor with a terrific clatter. These included the items she'd stolen at the railway station plus the ones from Chisbury's store, plus all the things she had stolen since then, on her rambles round Chisleton.

'Over here,' Super Gran called to the others as they looked up.

So now they knew where to look for the missing key. But they still couldn't find it as Hatty had slipped it inside the earth of a potted plant she had stolen from Poshtown station.

'Got it!' Super Gran said, after using her X-ray vision to locate it, in desperation.

'Right, then, Batty Hatty Patti,' Dumpling said, 'let's be having you inside this cell . . . Huh?'

He swung round – but Hatty was gone. She had scarpered, unnoticed, while the search was going on! And Dustin had scarpered along with her!

'Coagulating koalas!' the Duchess exclaimed. 'That Fatty Catty must've let Bruce out while we weren't looking.'

'Come on, Duchess,' Super Gran said, 'I'll take you along to the mayor and the race.'

'Rightio, Scottie,' she said, as they left the office, 'I want to be there bang on time to start it.'

At the grassy area in the High Street where the Pigeon Race would start and finish, the mayor and the chief race official, Alf Fishal, were having words.

'Where's that Aussie Duchess got to?' the mayor asked. 'She was supposed to arrive at the Town Hall hours ago. She's due to start the race.'

'I've got enough to do to get these race entrants organized without worrying about your precious Duchess,' Alf said. 'If you don't let me get on with this there won't *be* a race to start!'

The thirty entrants clustered around him with their birds and Alf, standing behind a long table full of check-sheets, pens, leg-tags and pigeon baskets, was doing his best to get everyone's pigeon registered.

'Who's first?' he asked.

'Me,' said Postman Pugh, his stuffed pigeon on his shoulder and the real one, Rosy Redlips, in her basket. 'Pugh,' he said, 'and Rosy Redlips.'

'Pugh. Rosy Redlips,' Alf repeated, marking the

names down on his check-sheets, then handing him a race-tag for the bird's leg.

'Next!' he said, as Pugh walked off and his wife, jealous Janet, fought her way through the crowd towards him, brandishing her favourite rolling-pin.

'Hey, Pugh-hoo . . .' she yelled as she struggled past the others in pursuit of her husband. 'Come back here! I want to nag you!'

The other pigeon fanciers lined up to register their birds, with the Scunner and Bony at the end of the queue, waiting to register Fast Lass for Newcastle Brown. Except, of course, that it was Chisbury which the Scunner had in his basket, in place of the stolen Fast Lass.

'We won't get away with it,' Bony whispered, glancing around nervously. 'We'll be rumbled.'

'Don't worry, we don't actually have to show the bird,' the Scunner assured him. 'The official knows it's in the basket and doesn't need to see it.'

'One of these fanciers must be the one who nicked Fast Lass,' Bony muttered, out of the side of his mouth. 'So that's one guy who knows this isn't her.'

'Aye, but he's not likely to tell, is he?' the Scunner pointed out, reasonably. ''Cos if he grasses on us – we'll grass on him!'

'Yeah, yeah, you're right,' Bony said, smiling with relief.

But he still looked nervous when their turn came and the Scunner declared in a confident voice that their pigeon was Fast Lass. He was brazening it out, although Bony was still worried that they'd be caught cheating.

The Scunner took the leg-tag which Alf gave him and he and Bony moved quickly off, away from the crowd, to get privacy to attach it to Chisbury's leg without anyone spotting what they were up to.

'Do we need to do this?' Bony asked. 'It seems a bit daft putting a tag on the leg of a dead pigeon!'

'Aye,' the Scunner agreed, 'but when it wins the race it'll have to have proof it was entered in the first place.'

'Yeah, I see,' said Bony, as the Scunner slipped Chisbury into his jacket pocket.

But Rott N. Scoundrel and his pupils who were in the crowd of spectators had been amazed to hear the Scunner registering Newcastle's pigeon.

'He registered Fast Lass – so what pigeon did you nick?' he asked Windy and Shorty.

'Dunno,' they replied, shrugging.

'Well, there's no point in worrying about it,' Scoundrel said. 'The best thing is for us to make use of this crowd – and get some pocket-picking practice!'

'Yeah, good idea,' the pupils agreed – and set to it.

And it was just about then, when the competitors were lining up and Alf was standing by with a starting pistol, that Super Gran arrived with the missing Duchess.

'The Duchess of Oz? At last!' the mayor greeted her. 'We've been searching all over for you.'

'Bouncing boomerangs!' she exclaimed. 'I was in your Pommy Police Station. I was a prison . . .'

'The Police Station?' the mayor interrupted. 'I never thought of looking there.'

'Bruce, I was a prison . . .' she continued.

But Super Gran didn't wait to hear the Duchess tell the mayor about her sojourn in one of his cells. She left them to it as she spotted Edison pushing her way through the crowd that had gathered for the start of the race.

'What're you doing here?' she asked.

'Willard sent me to look for you and take you back to the match. Where have you been?'

'It's a long story. I'll tell you on the way back.'

But then she saw the mayor and the Duchess climbing the steps to a little platform.

'Wait a wee minute, lassie. We might as well see the start of the race, seeing as we're here, eh?'

'Well O K,' Edison said, grudgingly. 'But we'd better not hang about or Willard'll go berserk.'

The mayor approached the microphone and cleared his throat.

'Ladies and gentlemen, welcome to this year's great Chisleton Pigeon Race, for which there are thirty entrants. I should now like to call on the Duchess of Oz, all the way from sunny Australia, to start the race for us.'

Super Gran looked at her watch. It was three o'clock exactly.

'Well, she managed to start it bang on time after all.'

'I declare this Pommy Pigeon Race open, darlings,' she said as she fired Alf Fishal's starting pistol in the air. 'And God bless all who sail in her!'

'Wow! It *was* bang on time!' Edison joked, putting her hands to her ears.

The Duchess had got her speeches mixed up in her excitement, but it didn't really matter as no one heard her over the noise of the pistol anyway!

At the sound of the gun each fancier opened his basket, releasing his bird. Except for the Scunner, of course, who had to shake the lid of his a few times and make some 'pigeon flapping' noises to cover the fact that Chisbury wasn't flying out of the basket but was lying in his pocket. Then, while everyone's attention was on the soaring pigeons, the two crooks slipped off through the crowd to put the Scunner's plan into action.

As Super Gran and Edison left, on their way to the match, the pigeons circled round a few times above the heads of the crowd.

'Jings, that's funny,' Super Gran said, stopping to stare up at them. 'The mayor said there were thirty pigeons in the race but my Super-vision tells me there's only twenty-nine birds up there.'

'Well, we haven't time to worry about it just now,' Edison told her, taking her by the arm and urging her towards the cricket ground. 'You've got a match to get back to.'

'Aye, you're right, lassie,' she agreed, as they hurried along the road. 'I've got to go and get the rest of

those wee snobby middens out for ducks, haven't I?'

'So, at the moment, you should be concentrating on ducks rather than pigeons!' Edison joked.

16   The Chisbury Chase!

When the race entrants and spectators saw the pigeons flying off in the direction of the park, heading out of Chisleton, they wandered away to have a look round the town until the birds returned at the end of the race.

And Alf Fishal and his assistant began operating Inventor Black's gadget which would ensure that the pigeons would fly in a circular course from Chisleton to Paddleton, to Poshtown, to Wallytown and then back to Chisleton again. This was achieved by a silent pigeon 'caller', attached to a radio-controlled model aircraft which flew ahead of the pigeons, persuading them to follow its silent 'tunes'.

But the Scunner and Bony had already hurried off into a back street to join the others, including the recently escaped Dustin.

'The last I heard of you you were being carried to the local nick by that old prune,' the Scunner said.

'Yeah, but I got away, didn't I?' replied the grinning Dustin. 'It was all down to Batty Hatty.'

'Where's she now?' Cedric asked.

'She's going round the crowd – picking their pockets!'

'That's enough chat,' the Scunner said. 'Let's get to work.'

He took Black's catapults out of his pockets and handed one each to the five men and then loaded Chisbury into the sixth one. He moved the gadget's control to 'Full Force' and his hand hovered over the 'On' switch.

'Here goes! You know what to do? Take up your positions!'

Bony headed for Newcastle's Poshe car parked near by, Dustin crouched down as if on an athlete's starting block, Cedric ran to the Scunner's trusty old car and Tub ran to his rusty old bike!

'He's off!' the Scunner yelled, as he pressed the lever which shot Chisbury out of the catapult and into the air, in the wake of the other twenty-nine pigeons.

And as the bird took off the Scunner's troops also took off. Bony zoomed away in the Poshe, Cedric shot off in the Scunner's car, Tub pedalled away on his bike and Dustin ran towards the river, still wearing his city suit and bowler hat and clutching his umbrella, which he'd remembered to nick back out of the nick!

Clyde remained with the Scunner and the two of them ran along the road following Chisbury's flight-path, in case it fell to earth too soon and had to be shot off again.

'Come on,' the Scunner yelled, 'it's heading over the park.'

As the bird whizzed overhead Newcastle Brown looked up at it. He was playing the piano on a low platform at his open-air concert, in front of a teenage audience.

'That must be a straggler,' he said. 'The others went over ages ago.'

Presently the Scunner and Clyde dashed through the park and approached the platform. Newcastle looked up at them and smiled.

'Hello, lads. How's Fast Lass doing?'

'Who?' said the Scunner.

He had forgotten about Newcastle's pigeon until Clyde nudged him violently in the back, making him reply: 'Oh, it's ... er ... she's ... um ... doing all right.'

Then, as Clyde passed the piano he leaned across the platform and, from force of habit, slammed the lid down on Newcastle's hands again!

As Super Gran and Edison reached the outside of the cricket ground Inventor Black came hurtling along in his wheelchair, looking agitated.

'Super Gran! Six of my mini-catapults have been stolen!'

'Jings, that's terrible, Blackie,' she sympathized.

'And not only that,' he continued, doing a wheelie and bringing his chair to a halt, 'they also pinched my dog flute. I can understand someone taking the cata-pults, but why the flute?'

'Look, Blackie,' Super Gran said, 'I've got to get back to this match and get on with my bowling. I'll try and track down the culprits later, OK?' And she rushed into the cricket ground.

'Come *on*, Gran,' Willard urged as he threw her the ball. 'We *need* you.'

'What's their score?' she asked, dreading the answer.

'One hundred and ten,' he replied, relieved that she had returned. 'And they only need forty-one to beat us.'

She took over from where she left off, by taking two wickets straight away.

'Whew!' Willard sighed with relief. He could relax slightly, now that his match-winning Gran was back.

But the wicket-taking didn't go on for long, for just then 'Tea-time' was announced and the umpires removed the bails.

'Well, that'll give me a wee break,' Super Gran said.

'A break, Gran?' Willard was astounded. 'But you've hardly been here all afternoon.'

She stopped walking off the pitch with the others, to put her hands on her hips, indignantly.

'Willie! I ask you! Don't you think I need a wee break from dashing all over the town? Apart from running up and down with all this bowling, not to mention getting those hundred and fifty runs for you?'

'OK, Gran, I forgot,' he said. 'You deserve a break.'

'I should think so, too!'

She put her arm around his shoulder and they walked in to join the others in the pavilion for their tea. Not that the Snobbers talked to any of them, they just sat in a corner by themselves and glowered at the Chisletonians.

'I wonder what they're plotting now?' she said, seeing Toff, Desmond and D. Red-Locks with their heads together, like three conspirators.

'They're probably just talking about the beating we're going to give them,' Willard said, smiling confidently. 'They've no chance of winning, not now you're back, Gran.'

'M'mm, I don't trust them,' she said, thoughtfully. 'I bet they're up to something.'

After flying over the park, Chisbury's flight continued towards the river.

It was Dustin's job to go after it on the first leg of the flight, but as Chisbury was liable to reach the river before he did he decided to 'borrow' a motorbike parked at the side of the road.

'Thanks,' he shouted, raising his bowler hat politely as he sped off on the bike.

'Hey! Come back here!' the furious motorcyclist yelled.

Dustin caught up with the pigeon as it reached the banks of the river. He was almost under it as it fell to the ground, the power of its catapult flight spent. But as he put his hands up to catch it, it hit him on his bowler hat, bounced off and landed on the back of a passing seagull flying towards the river.

'Huh?' he exclaimed as Chisbury fell off the gull's back and landed in the water. 'Oh, no!'

He looked round for some means of reaching the floating bird and spotted a rowing-boat moored to the river bank.

'This'll do,' he muttered as he pushed it out and scrambled aboard. 'Thanks.'

He raised his bowler hat to the boat's owner, then he rowed out into the middle of the river to fish Chisbury out with the handle of his rolled umbrella.

'Hey! My boat!' the angry boatman yelled.

Dustin shook the water off the pigeon, took his catapult out and shot it skywards towards Paddleton, where, according to the Scunner's calculations, the next flight would take it.

And he was correct, as Tub, having reached there on his bike, could confirm. The only trouble was that the pigeon unsportingly landed on the outskirts of the town, in the middle of a swamp!

'Oh, no!' Tub moaned, jumping off the bike and plunging through the gooey, sticky morass to retrieve it. 'Yeugh! Ugh!'

Eventually he reached it, pulled it out of the boggy mess and wiped some of the dirt off on his sleeve. Then he pulled his catapult out of his pocket and shot Chisbury off again, towards Poshtown, its next expected port of call.

And once again the Scunner's calculations were almost spot on, for it landed there as Cedric jumped out of the Scunner's car to catch it. But the trouble this time was that Chisbury chose to come down on top of a ten-storey building!

'Curses!' Cedric muttered.

But he cursed even harder when he discovered the lift was out of order and he had to climb the ten flights of stairs to retrieve it!

'Huh . . . huh . . . huh . . .' he said, breathlessly, when he finally reached the roof and saw Chisbury lying there, grinning up at him cheekily. Or at least that's how it appeared to him!

He pulled out his catapult, loaded Chisbury and sent it flying at full force towards Wallytown.

And once again the pigeon landed on target – almost. Bony, lounging against Newcastle's Poshe, awaiting the bird's arrival, was surprised to see how close it came to its predicted landing site.

'I've got to hand it to the Scunner,' he murmured. 'That was pretty close. Amazing!'

But he wasn't quite so full of praise when Chisbury landed in a mass of rough, prickly bushes which he had to scramble through to retrieve it. And he, like the others, ended up cursing the instigator of this stupid flight-plan.

'Why did I get involved in this crackpot scheme?' he muttered.

Eventually, with his face and hands scratched and his clothes torn, he found it. Then, after removing the mud and pieces of foliage with his handkerchief, he produced his catapult and sent the bird hurtling into the sky once more, towards the Townhead district of Chisleton, where the Scunner had instructed them all to rendezvous. Then he climbed back into the Poshe and drove there.

The Scunner and Clyde were the first ones to arrive at Townhead, having had less distance to travel than the others. But on their way there, running through the park again, they passed Newcastle, who was still performing at his concert.

'I wonder how Chisbury's getting on,' the Scunner said, looking skywards.

'Who's Chisbury?' Newcastle asked, as he tinkled his electronic piano's plastic ivories.

'Er . . . ah . . . um . . . who?' the Scunner stammered, caught out.

'The Who?' Newcastle laughed. 'What's a rock group got to do with it?' Then he added: 'How's Fast Lass doing?'

The Scunner stopped to think about all this and Clyde, catching up with him, nudged him in the back, making him say:

'Oh, Fast Lass? *That* Fast Lass? Oh, she's doing fine.'

'Hey! Gerrout the way, Grandads!' the teenage audience yelled angrily at the men who blocked their view of the pop star.

'This is my request spot,' Newcastle told them. 'Have you any requests?'

'Yeah,' growled the opera-loving Clyde, 'give it a rest!'

And he slammed the lid down on Newcastle's fingers again!

17   The Scunner's Predicament

The Scunner and Clyde had been waiting in Townhead for some time when Chisbury arrived, as expected. Its rocket-powered flight had resulted in its getting ahead of the main batch of pigeons and it reached there a few minutes before them. It landed on the road and the Scunner ran to pick it up and shove it into his pocket before curious passersby wondered what the mysterious object was that fell from the skies!

Presently Tub, the Muscles and Bony – wet, mud-splattered and exhausted – joined the Scunner and Clyde, as arranged.

Townhead, about half a mile from Chisleton High Street, was in the pigeons' direct flight-path. And the place the Scunner had chosen as a rendezvous was a building site – cluttered with materials, rubble and debris – beside a row of houses.

'The workers are having a day off to go to the Pigeon Race,' he explained. 'So we'll have the place to ourselves.'

'But how are you going to make sure Chisbury wins the race?' Bony asked. 'I mean, if you shoot it off too soon it'll arrive long before the other pigeons, and that'll be suspicious. But on the other hand if you wait too long they'll fly past us and reach the finishing line before Chisbury takes off.'

By way of an answer the Scunner walked over to his car, parked near the building site, took out five pigeon baskets and six children's fishing-nets and handed the men a net each.

'When they fly towards us we catch them in the nets and whip them into the baskets. Brilliant, eh?'

'Yeah, but those little perishers are flying too high for us to reach with the nets,' Bony pointed out.

'But that's where yon wee dog flute comes in handy.' The Scunner turned to Cedric and put his hand out. 'Have you still got it, Ceddie?'

'Yeah, Boss,' Cedric said, pulling it from his pocket and handing it over.

'Look, Uncle,' Tub said, pointing to a black cloud in the distance. 'Here they come!'

'Just in time,' the Scunner said, and blew the whistle.

The effect was immediate. Twenty-eight birds came swooping down out of the sky towards them and did little aerial dances a few metres above the ground. Then the six men dashed around, catching them in their nets as they hovered obligingly.

'I wonder what music the whistle played?' mused Clyde, the music-lover.

'Maybe it was "Sparrow in the tree top",' Tub said, repeating Edison's earlier suggestion.

'Naw,' said Clyde, 'it was more likely to be the ballet music, "The Two Pigeons"!'

'Never mind about the bally music, just get the bally birds into the baskets,' the Scunner snapped.

All six of them gingerly lifted the captured pigeons out of the nets and placed them in the baskets' separate compartments, which kept them apart.

The Scunner smiled, pleased with himself. His plan had worked perfectly. He'd be able to collect his fee from Newcastle as well as his diplomas from Scoundrel's College.

'Is that the lot?' he asked as he counted them.

'No, there's one missing,' Bony said. 'We've only got twenty-eight.'

'It won't matter,' Cedric – the pigeon expert! – assured them. 'There's sometimes stragglers in races.'

But the missing pigeon, Postman Pugh's Rosy Redlips – the slowest bird in the race – flew past them unnoticed while they were busy putting the others in the baskets.

'Right,' said the Scunner, 'we've just to shoot good old Chisbury towards the finishing line now.'

He pulled it from his pocket and loaded it into the catapult for its final flight.

'Then we'll wait for a wee while before we let the others go,' he added, 'to make sure it gets a head start.'

He sent it off with just enough of the catapult's force to get it to the High Street. Then, after waiting a few minutes, the men each opened a basket and released the other pigeons.

'O K,' he said, 'let's get back to the High Street and pick up Newcastle's winnings for him!' He turned to the Muscles. 'You two can travel in my car.'

'No, thanks,' said Cedric as he and Dustin joined Bony and Clyde in Newcastle's car. 'We've never been in a Poshe before.'

'Yeah,' Dustin added, eagerly, 'we're gonna travel in style.'

'Hey, don't leave me with all these baskets,' the Scunner moaned as they zoomed off in the Poshe, and Tub pedalled after them on his bike.

He threw the nets and baskets into the back seat of his car. Then, smiling happily that his plans had been a complete success, he decided on a little celebration. He pulled from his pocket the cigar that Newcastle had given him for this very occasion and leaned against the car as he unwrapped it and lit it. He was going to enjoy this. That's what he thought!

There was a sudden explosion. Unknown to him the pop star, who was fond of a practical joke – as long as he wasn't the victim of it! – had given him a trick cigar. The Scunner, his face blackened by its soot, cursed him.

'Huh, very funny – I don't think.'

But then he made his big mistake. He threw away the cigar and it landed in among the builders' rubble, which contained a leaking gas canister.

There was a burst of flame and he leapt to escape, but tripped over some bricks, fell headlong and got his feet caught in a coil of wire, which trapped him.

'Help! Tub! Muscles!' he yelled.

But by now they were well on their way to the High Street and couldn't hear him. He was on his own.

He watched the flames lick nearer to himself *and* to his car – which might explode at any minute.

'Curses!' he muttered. 'Why did this happen when I'm so near success?' Then he yelled: 'Mum! Save me, SAVE ME!'

The Scunner's Mum didn't come to his aid but someone else's did! His plight had been spotted by one of the neighbours, Mrs Bowler, the wife of the cricket umpire.

'Help! Tub! Muscles!' he repeated.

'You'll need muscles to get you out of that,' she agreed, as she popped her head out of her window. 'And I know the very ones – Super Gran's!'

'No, not that old crone-bag,' he gasped, 'get the Fire Brigade. They'll know what to do.'

'But she'll get here before them,' she said, as she popped her head back inside the window.

'What, Super "Thingy" faster than the Fire Brigade? Never.'

She rushed to phone the cricket pavilion.

'This is Mrs Bowler, the umpire's wife. I've got an urgent message to put over your Public Address System.'

'Go ahead,' said the man who answered, pressing the switch on the PA system and holding the phone receiver against its microphone.

'Super Gran! Help! SOS! Rescue! Fire at building site! Townhead!'

'Oh no, not again!' Willard groaned.

The match had recently resumed, Super Gran had

got another two batsmen out and the Snobbers still needed their forty-one runs.

'I'll have to go,' she said.

'But if you go the Snobbers'll get the runs they need and we'll lose the match. Stay,' he pleaded. 'Just ignore it, Gran.'

'Don't you dare ignore it!' cut in Mr Bowler, whose wife, he thought, was in danger. 'She must be in dire straits.'

'Dire Straits?' Willard muttered. 'What's a pop group got to do with it?'

'I'm off!' she insisted, and rushed from the pitch. But as she ran Mrs Bowler continued her appeal:

'S O S – Save our Scunner . . .'

'What, the Scunner?' Williard yelled. 'Hey, Gran, stop! Let him stay put.'

'What a thing to say! It doesn't matter *who* is in danger: I must help them. Even if it *is* that wee bachle.'

She continued to rush from the ground and, outside, spotted a passing taxi. She leapt aboard it without giving the driver time to stop. Then, after swinging the passenger door open and clambering aboard, she asked:

'D'you know a building site in Townhead, cabbie?'

'Yes.'

'Then drive there! Quickly! There's a fire!'

He put his foot down and weaved his vehicle in and out of the traffic, while ahead of them the flames crept closer to the Scunner's vehicle.

'If it reaches the petrol tank it's kerPOW!' he moaned. 'The end of the Scunner and my ambitions to be the world's greatest crook. Curse that rotten cigar for putting me into this vile predicament.'

Mrs Bowler dived out of her front door towards him. 'Don't worry, I've sent for Super Gran!'

'Oh, no, not that old petrified prune!'

At the thought of *her* rescuing him, and the utter shame of it, he struggled to free himself from the wire, without success. And Mrs Bowler also tried to free him, but also without success.

Suddenly the taxi appeared, screeched to a halt and Super Gran leapt out. His face lit up with relief. Despite what he'd said about her, he was glad to see her.

'Save your dear old pal,' he wailed.

'What – you? You've never been my dear old anything – but I'll save you anyway! I'd rescue anyone – even you, you wee bachle!'

She took a deep breath and Super-blew the flames out, extinguishing them completely in seconds. Then she freed him from the wire wound round his ankles.

Mrs Bowler and the taxi driver applauded this and Super Gran made the Scunner pay for her taxi fare. Then, as the cab drove away, Mrs Bowler said:

'I told you Super Gran would rescue you from your predicament, didn't I?'

'But what *I'd* like to know,' Super Gran said, 'is how you came to be in the predicament in the first place. What're you doing here in Townhead? Eh?'

'Well . . . er . . . ah . . . um . . . you see,' he stam-

mered, not wanting to reveal anything about Chisbury and the Pigeon Race.

'Come on – tell me!' she demanded.

She grabbed him by the jacket and shook him so hard that the catapult and dog flute jumped out of his pocket!

'Aha!' she said.

'Aha?' he asked. 'What's a pop group got to do with it?'

'Aha!' she repeated, recognizing the items as belonging to Inventor Black.

'Yoo-hoo!' she exclaimed.

'Yoo-hoo?' he echoed, puzzled.

'Aye, yoo-hoo. It was,' she explained, 'you who – stole those gadgets from Blackie, wasn't it?'

Then she looked inside his car and spotted the pigeon baskets and fishing-nets.

'Oh, and what are these, eh?'

'Well . . . er . . . ah . . . um . . .'

'Never mind.' She pushed him into the passenger's seat. 'You can tell me on the way back to the High Street.'

And she jumped into the driver's seat, waved goodbye to Mrs Bowler and zoomed the car through the streets at a furious speed.

18 Winners and Losers

When Newcastle finished his concert he carried his portable piano back to the High Street to await the end of the race. And he was surprised, as everyone in the crowd was, when only one bird, Chisbury, suddenly dropped out of the sky and landed at his feet.

'Fast Lass!' he yelled. 'I've won!'

But Alf Fishal picked up the pigeon and stared at it.

'Wait a minute,' he said, suspiciously, 'that was a funny sort of landing!'

'Yes,' his assistant agreed. 'She looked as if she'd been shot out of a catapult!'

Alf inspected the bird's race-tag and checked his race-sheets. 'Yes, it's Fast Lass all right. She seems to be O K – but asleep!'

'I've won,' Newcastle repeated, and although he was smiling he seemed a bit puzzled by it all.

'Look,' one of the pigeon fanciers said, pointing to the sky, 'here's the rest of them.'

And leading the way was little Rosy Redlips!

'That's mine,' Pugh yelled, jumping with excitement. 'My little Rosy. Who'd've thought she'd come in second. I didn't think she'd even finish the course, let alone come in second.'

Little did he know her success was entirely due to

the other – faster! – birds being held back, and not to Rosy's racing ability.

'Huh! That's one in the eye to you, Janet,' he said to his wife as she advanced on him through the crowd, her rolling-pin at the ready. 'I wasn't wasting my time after all.'

'Uh?' She was speechless.

Just then Bony and the others arrived in the High Street and joined the pigeon fanciers, officials and spectators to see Newcastle being presented with the race trophy, full of tenners.

'Here you are, Bruce,' the Duchess of Oz said. 'Your birdie's a real little beaut. Even if she *is* a bit tired! But may I say how truly delighted I am to be here in your fair dinkum town of . . .'

But Alf Fishal interrupted the Duchess's speech by only just noticing something strange about the race winner.

'She's not asleep – she's dead!' he gasped.

'But how could a dead pigeon win a race?' his assistant asked.

'And she seems to have been frozen!' Alf added.

'What?' Newcastle said in a shocked voice. 'Dead? Fast Lass? I know she was poorly, but . . .'

He stopped before he said too much and gave himself away.

Bony, seeing that the Scunner hadn't yet arrived, took it upon himself to be the spokesman.

'It . . . um . . . *she* died of excitement at winning the race,' he explained as he snatched the bird from Alf, to hide it.

153

'Yes, but she was frozen!' Alf pointed out.

'Ah ... well, that was caused,' Bony said, 'er ... um ... by the high altitude it ... um ... *she* was flying at!'

No one believed him, especially the pigeon fanciers whose birds were now beginning to land, but while everyone argued about it the Scunner's car appeared and screeched to a halt. Super Gran leapt out, hauling the cigar-blackened villain with one hand towards the officials, while carrying a fishing-net and a pigeon basket in the other hand, as evidence.

'Super Gran, you "wee" Scottish beaut,' the Duchess said with a smile. 'If that's a race entry you've got you're too late – the race's over!'

'Look at the state *I'm* in!' the Scunner stormed. 'Where's that Newcastle? I'm gonna kill him!'

But Alf Fishal was still suspicious of the whole thing.

'Something funny's going on,' he said.

'Aye, something funny's going on, so it is,' Super Gran agreed, giving him the net and the basket. 'I found the Scunner with these, at Townhead.'

She suddenly grabbed Chisbury from Bony's hand, turned it over and then quickly flipped it back again.

'What's this?' she said. '"Weight one pound. Thaw two hours before eating"!'

'You silly twit,' Bony yelled at the Scunner, 'you forgot to remove the deep freeze label from Chisbury. Trust you to make a right mess of the whole thing.'

'Oh, so you admit this is a supermarket bird, do you?' she said, turning to the Scunner.

154

'Och, it was all Tub's fault, the silly wee nyaff,' he replied, but Tub merely shrugged.

'This must be the only pigeon from a deep freeze ever to win a race,' she joked and the crowd laughed.

Then she admitted:

'I told a wee white lie. The bird doesn't have a label!' She showed them its bare back. 'But it got these crooks here to confess. You see, I read the Scunner's mind as we were driving here, but I wanted a confession from him, too, and I got it.'

'Right, that's it,' said Alf Fishal, 'I officially declare Fast Lass – or Chisbury, or whatever you call it! – disqualified. And the bird that came second is now declared the winner.'

'That's Rosy Redlips!' screamed Pugh, happily. He was over the proverbial moon. His bird had won the great Chisleton Pigeon Race! 'Yippee!'

Janet, no longer jealous of the other bird in her prize-winning husband's life, threw away her rolling-pin. Then she threw her arms around his neck and gave him a big sloppy kiss. 'Sploosh!'

'Huh?' he said, surprised.

The rolling-pin flew over the heads of the crowd and landed behind them. But it didn't lie on the ground for long. A woman's hand snatched it up and thrust it inside her huge black cloak to join the other stolen items in there. Then Batty Hatty slipped quietly away towards the station, her day's work done!

But Scoundrel and his pupils, after the lucrative

afternoon they'd had at the crowd's expense, weren't too happy with Hatty.

'Hey,' Bill yelled, 'those wallets we nicked have been nicked!'

'Oh no!' Scoundrel said, checking his pocket. 'Worse than that – my *own* wallet's been nicked!'

'Yeah, well, whoever did it certainly doesn't need any of *your* lessons, that's for sure!' Wally moaned.

And Newcastle Brown wasn't too happy either as he turned to Bony to demand:

'What's happened to Fast Lass? Eh?'

'I dunno,' Bony shrugged.

But Tub suddenly pointed to the top of Newcastle's piano where a pigeon was happily dancing around.

'Where did she come from?' Newcastle asked.

'The pigeon fancier who nicked her has put her back,' the Scunner said. 'She's not a threat, now that the race's over.'

No one saw who returned her but the men whose birds came in second and third behind Rosy Redlips were full of smiles, so it was assumed that one of them was the culprit.

'It doesn't matter who it was,' the depressed Scunner pointed out, 'Newcastle . . . er . . . Mr Brown's Fast Lass – or Chisbury! – was disqualified anyway. So he didn't win anything.'

But Newcastle was smiling – and he shouldn't have been, if he wasn't a winner.

'Fast Lass was ill recently and had no chance of winning,' he confessed. 'That's why I was amazed when

we thought she'd won – and I nearly gave the show away! Anyway, I didn't bet on her, I bet on the pigeons that came in second and third. So I've won that much, even if I didn't win the race. So *I'm* happy.'

He turned to Clyde. 'Go and collect my winnings, will you.'

He put Fast Lass into her basket and placed it in his Poshe, ready to leave.

'Would you like to have Chisbury,' the Scunner said, offering it, 'as a souvenir?'

'No, you keep it. You never know, it might come in handy for another race!' he laughed.

Clyde returned with Newcastle's winnings and the Scunner was given his share.

'We'll see you at next year's race, eh, Scunner?' Bony said.

'No fear! I've had enough of rotten pigeons *and* rotten exploding cigars!'

'Well I did say you'd get blackened, didn't I?' Bony laughed.

'And does that mean you're giving the birds a miss from now on?' Newcastle asked.

'I know one old bird I *always* give a miss, if I can,' the Scunner retorted. 'That old battle-axe Super Gran.'

'Yeah, talking of which,' Bony said, 'where's she got to?'

'She's gone back to that cricket match Mr Chop was going to,' Dustin said, grinning his usual grin.

'Oh aye, I'd forgotten about Chop,' the Scunner

admitted. 'Pity we didn't get hold of *his* cash, isn't it? Still, we've got our share of Newcastle ... er ... Mr Brown's winnings.'

'Oh, go on,' Newcastle relented, 'call me Newcastle.'

'Oh, thanks, Newcastle,' the Scunner gushed.

Bony now jumped into the front passenger seat of the Poshe and Clyde climbed into the back seat. Then Newcastle leaned in and thumped his electronic piano down hard on Clyde's knees, in revenge for all the sore fingers he'd suffered at Clyde's hands!

'Ouch!'

Then he climbed into the Poshe and it roared off out of Chisleton as he, Bony and Clyde waved goodbye to the Scunner and company.

19 Super Gran's LEFT Bowling!

Super Gran left the crowd at the Pigeon Race to race back to the cricket match – once again!

'The Snobbers' score's one hundred and forty-six!' Muggins yelled at her as she rushed past him.

'Jings!'

'They only need a four to equal our score,' he added.

'And a six to win,' Leekie said, worriedly.

She headed for the pitch to get the ball from Willard and resume her bowling but as she passed Desmond, loitering near the boundary, she didn't notice him sticking his foot out.

'Ouch!' she cried as she fell headlong on to the grass and landed on her right wrist, twisting it. 'Ow-ow!'

'Gran!'

'Super Gran!'

Her team-mates crowded round her, to see how badly she was injured and to help her to her feet. Behind them D. Red-Locks and his partner, the last two batsmen at the wicket, sniggered at her misfortune. And from the steps of the pavilion the rest of the Snobbers could be heard laughing loudly.

'Oh dear, I hope you didn't hurt yourself, Dessy?'

Timothy said, as Desmond skipped lightly up the steps. The others joined in the sniggering.

'Well, yes, I did sustain a minuscule bump,' he admitted. 'I may have to walk with a limp, now.'

'Oh, don't say that, old chap,' Timothy sympathized, as the Snobbers gathered round the fraudulent Desmond and pretended to comfort him, guffawing like mad.

While, on the pitch, Super Gran, the real injured party, said:

'It's my wrist. I've wrenched it. I can't bowl with it. Sorry, Willie. Sorry, boys.'

Now they really had a problem. Should she *not* bowl what could possibly be the last ball of the match and give the Snobbers a great chance to win? Or should she try to bowl with her left arm?

'If you don't mind, peasants,' Timothy shouted, snootily, 'may we continue with the game? Now that you've all managed to get the old bag of bones back on her spindly legs again!'

'The cheeky wee poultice!' she stormed. 'I'll show him! Gimme that ball, Willie!'

'Are you *going* to bowl with your left arm, Gran?'

'I sure am,' she said determinedly, marching on to the pitch while the others took up their fielding positions again. 'I'd bowl with my teeth if I had to, to get those snobby wee hoodlums out!'

'But have you ever bowled with your left arm?' Willard asked.

'No, but I'd never even bowled with my *right* arm

161

until yesterday, so I suppose I could learn to use my left one.'

'Yeah, but you haven't time to practise! This might be the last ball of the match!'

As Willard took up his position Super Gran ran up and bowled, awkwardly and lop-sidedly, with her left hand. Then she watched in horror as D. Red-Locks thumped it high in the air, over her head, towards the boundary, where it only had to land and roll across the line for the Snobbers to equal the Chisleton score – or sail over it for an outright win.

But she didn't hang about. She zoomed off towards the boundary, passing the other fielders who were vainly trying to chase the skyed ball and guess where it would land.

It soared onwards and upwards as she pursued it. Then, about half a metre from the line, it dropped to earth. And it could still either be a four or a six – or nothing, if she caught it!

She threw herself at the ball and awkwardly thrust her left hand towards it. She grabbed at it, mere centimetres from the line, and rolled over on to her back. But she'd caught it and D. Red-Locks was out. His whole team was out. Chisleton had won by four runs and the match was over – at last!

The team clustered round her, slapping her back and cheering her. And as they left the pitch Muggins, Leekie, Chop and the other spectators gave her a standing ovation.

'Good old Super Gran,' they yelled.

'Super Gran triumphs again!' Edison shouted.

And while the Chisletonians celebrated their win the disgusted Snobbers quietly slunk away with their tail between their legs. They didn't even wait to change out of their whites – they couldn't board their minibus and speed away quickly enough!

The Scunner was smiling as he waved Newcastle's bundle of tenners with one hand and drove his car with the other.

'For once, lads, we've been successful,' he said, smiling.

'But where are we going, Uncle?' Tub asked.

'To the Crooks' College for our diplomas. We've not only completed the course but also outwitted all the other pupils, by pulling their jobs. My heartiest congratulations, lads.'

But they were taken aback when they reached the college to find the doors locked, the windows shuttered and no sign of life.

'What's that?' Cedric asked, pointing to a note pinned to the front door.

'"Rott N. Scoundrel can be contacted at Chisleton Police Station",' the Scunner read out loud. 'Oh-oh, it looks as if he's been nicked. We'll just have to go *there* and see him.'

'Not me,' said Dustin, 'I'm a fu . . . a fugi . . . a fugit . . . an outlaw!'

'Aye, I forgot you'd just escaped from their cells. You're right, you'd better stay out of their way.'

The others arrived at the Police Station to find that Scoundrel had been arrested by Dumpling and was being led, in handcuffs, to the cells.

'What's the charge?' the Scunner asked.

'You may well ask!' Scoundrel said. 'Just listen to this!'

'The only one I've been able to find,' Dumpling replied as he pointed to an old, dusty book lying open on the desk, 'is an old medieval Chisleton by-law which states that "ye felon did sette up ye schule for ye knavish crookes without ye official permit".'

'Is that all?' The Scunner was astonished.

'Yes, but when Inspector Muggins gets back from the cricket match I'm sure he'll be able to think of a better charge.'

'Er . . . Mr Scoundrel . . . ah . . . before you're in your cell – where you'll be in yirsel',' – he giggled at his Scottish joke – 'could I ask you to give me the two diplomas I'm entitled to?'

'What two diplomas?' asked Scoundrel, turning at the cell doorway as he entered.

'One for completing the course and one for using my initiative in stealing the jobs of the other pupils' groups.'

But before Scoundrel could reply, Muggins, Leekie and the other policemen returned from the match, along with Super Gran, Willard and Edison. And they were all wearing the happy, smiling faces that only a winning team would wear.

'We won!' Leekie yelled, needlessly.

The newcomers trooped into the main area of the station but stopped on seeing the Scunner and company there, and the arrested Scoundrel in his cell. A Press photographer entered behind the others and began photographing everyone in sight, while his mate, a reporter, began interviewing Dumpling.

'I need details about your exploits,' he said. 'I believe you're a bit of a hero?'

Dumpling, standing beside Scoundrel's cell, smiled proudly. 'Did you hear about the Duchess of Oz?' he asked.

'That was a wrongful arrest, wasn't it?' the reporter said as he wrote something into his notebook.

'Er, yes,' Dumpling admitted. 'But I also arrested Dustin, one of the Muscles.'

'Ah, he was the one who escaped, wasn't he?' the reporter reminded him.

'Er . . . ah . . . um . . . yes, so he was,' Dumpling said, then brightened. 'But then there was Batty Hatty Patti.'

'And she was the one who *let* him escape, wasn't she?'

Dumpling was getting desperate. Surely there was *one* success among that day's many arrests? He couldn't think who it was until Scoundrel put his handcuffed hands through the bars and tugged Dumpling's sleeve. 'Remember me?'

'Oh yes, I forgot,' Dumpling said, smiling. 'There's Scoundrel, of course.'

'Ah, success at last!' the reporter remarked, drily.

The photographer pushed his way through the crowd to photograph Dumpling as he posed in front of the cell, with Scoundrel in the background.

But while this was going on Muggins was addressing the Scunner.

'Did I hear you asking for some diplomas?'

'Aye, that's right,' the Scunner said, and was totally taken aback when Muggins laughed loudly.

'The only diploma *you* deserve,' he said through his laughter, 'is one from *me* – to say you're the world's worst crook!'

This was the cruellest insult the Scunner could be given.

'Yeah,' Scoundrel shouted, 'and there's no way you'll even get *one* diploma.'

'Why not?' the peeved Scunner asked.

'You stole the other pupils' jobs, but you didn't do what you were told to do.'

'What was that?'

'You didn't steal any hubcaps! You couldn't even do *that*!' He snorted. 'There's one thing the Inspector and I agree on – you *are* the world's worst crook!'

20 Shocks and Scares
for the Scunner!

The newspaper reporter turned his attention to Muggins.

'PC Dumpling's been here on a trial period, I believe?'

'Yes, but . . .'

'Would you say, in view of the mixed success of his various arrests, you'd be willing to keep him on here in the Chisleton Police Force?'

'Er . . . ah . . . um . . . ah . . . possibly,' Muggins replied.

It wasn't a definite yes, but Dumpling was so pleased that it wasn't a definite no that he threw his arms round Muggins's neck and hugged him, much to the man's embarrassment.

'Gerroff!' he muttered, blushing furiously.

Just then the door of the Police Station opened and Mr Chop entered. He pushed his way through the crowd to reach the Scunner at the far side of the room.

'Dustbin told me you were here and I just had to thank you,' he said, waving a huge bundle of banknotes at him.

'What for?' the puzzled Scunner asked.

'This!' said Chop. 'It's the profit I've made – in just

one day! – from that information about Stocks and Shares you gave Dustbin, to pass on to me.'

'What information?' The Scunner had forgotten all about it.

'Funny,' Chop said, thoughtfully, 'you'd think *Dustbin* would talk *rubbish*! But this time he was talking sense!'

'What d'you mean?' the Scunner said.

'I took his advice – *your* advice – and did what he suggested and I made a "killing" on the Stock Market. Thank you ever so much. Thank you, thank you, thank you!'

He fought his way back through the crowd again to leave the station, leaving the Scunner having a nervous breakdown!

'What!' he screamed. 'I had a means of making money and I passed it on to Dustbin, I mean Dustin, who passed it on to Chop – who's made a fortune. And I've missed out on it. Yeee-eeeks!'

While he tore handfuls of his hair out in rage, he furiously racked his brains to remember what the information was he had passed on. Suddenly the doors burst open and Dustin appeared in the doorway, behind the rest of the people in the crowded room.

'Hey, Dustbin – I mean, Dustin,' the Scunner shouted, 'can you remember what . . .'

But before he could tax Dustin's dim, dusty memory by asking him to recall what the Stocks and Shares nonsense had been, Leekie sprang into action. He realized that a fugitive from justice was in their midst.

'Get 'im, men,' he yelled.

Dustin turned and fled, with Leekie and the other policemen in hot pursuit, and this rather emptied the Police Station.

Super Gran now turned to the broken-hearted, memory-racking Scunner, to console him.

'Cheer up, money isn't everything.'

'It is to me, haggis-face,' he retorted.

Then Tub opened his mouth – and put his foot in it!

'But you don't need that money, Uncle. You've got the cash from Newcastle's race winnings.'

'Belt up,' the Scunner warned him, but too late. Muggins had heard him and demanded to see what Tub was talking about.

'Here,' the Scunner snarled, pulling the wad of banknotes from his pocket.

Muggins grabbed them.

'These'll make up for all the trouble friend Dustbin caused,' he said. 'Poor old Dumpling was nearly a frozen dumpling!'

'But you can't confiscate that cash,' the Scunner said. 'I know my rights.'

'I'm not,' Muggins said, smiling. 'I'm merely accepting a kind, generous donation from you for the Chisleton Police Benevolent Fund.'

The Scunner gnashed his teeth.

'Curse you and your big mouth, Tub,' he said as he removed his hat and hit Tub over the head with it. 'And curse my rotten memory,' he added. 'What on earth was all that nonsense we told Chop? If only I could remember it . . .'

He suddenly had another good idea and turned to Super Gran.

'You could read my mind and find out what that Stocks and Shares nonsense was! And that's *not* against the law!'

'You mean,' she said, smiling, 'that you'd consider a ploy that wasn't against the law? Amazing!'

'If you do it I'll go half-ers on the proceeds with you,' he said, pleading.

But before Super Gran could reply, the doors burst open again and the Duchess of Oz popped her head in.

'Hello, Pommy darlings,' she greeted them with a smile. 'I seem to have mislaid your truly dinkum railway station. Can any of you help me find it?'

'Sorry, Scunner,' Super Gran said as she headed towards the Duchess and took Willard and Edison with her, 'but it looks as if it's Super Gran to the rescue again. Tattie-bye . . .'

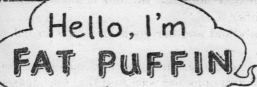